CONTENTS

HER SCANDALOUSLY ENTANGLED HEART

The Balfour Hotel Book 4

AMANDA DAVIS

When a beautiful guest arrives at the hotel, she has clearly arrived under a cloud of pretense, but what motive does she have for deception?

To Samuel, the maitre d' of the Balfour Hotel, it is obvious that the newly arrived guest, Miss Lorna Hastings, is not who she claims. Samuel finds himself in a precarious position—torn between his loyalty to his employers, the Balfours, and the comely young woman who awakens every protective instinct he possesses.

Why he feels the need to chivalrously come to the aid of Miss Hastings, he's uncertain. Perhaps he feels a kinship towards her because he, too has dark secrets he prefers to keep hidden.

Or, perhaps his motives have more to do with matters of the heart.

PROLOGUE

He stared forlornly out the window of his bedchamber hearing the raised voice of his father and the meek replies of his mother. They had been squabbling for hours, not an uncommon occurrence in the household. But, to Santos, their arguments seemed more frequent lately.

Perhaps he was merely more aware of the endless woes that plagued his father, Rafael, or the plaintive cries of his mother, who knew not how to right the wrongs of years past. Wrongs, as far as Santos could tell, that had little to do with her at all.

The boy was but eight years old, but he knew enough about the ways of marriage to understand that he would never be party to such a terrible union. Why, his father and mother could barely seem to stand being in the same room together. Santos could not fathom how they had ever come to wed.

His brother thought of him romantic, foolish, but Santos swore he would never live in such an untenable household once he was grown.

As if reading his younger brother's mind, Joaquin slipped inside the rooms, unannounced, and joined Santos at the window seat, a deep sigh escaping his lips.

"I fear one day he will kill her if only with his harsh words," the older boy told Santos. "He is far too cruel at times. Far too cruel."

Santos wanted to agree with his sibling, but he could not bring himself to speak ill of his father. The commandments dictated that he was to respect his parents, and Santos was nothing if not obedient to the commandments. Even if he did concede that his father could be unbearably harsh.

"You say nothing!" Joaquin barked, disappointed that Santos had not sided with him. "Have you lost your tongue?"

There was nothing the boy could say. To defy his father for the sake of appeasing his brother was a difficult choice. Santos was saved his own response when the voice in the neighboring chamber escalated. It was then that Santos heard the words that would change his life as he knew it. Although, when he later considered them, he realized he must have heard them many times before.

"You have ruined my future!" his father screamed at his mother. "I was cheated out of the life I deserve!"

A strangled sob reverberated through Santos's ears, and he stared at his older brother with confusion.

"What does he mean he was cheated?" Santos heard himself query, although as he spoke, he wished he had not. The sneer on Joaquin's face was one Santos knew too well—it belonged to his father. It radiated a smugness, an arrogance, that Santos lacked.

"You do not know?" Joaquin jeered. "You do not know how we could have lived in luxury and wealth?"

Santos did not know what to make of such nonsense. They were not of noble steed, regardless of the airs Rafael Conostoga attempted to present to their peers. He half suspected his brother was mocking, but there was an intense glint in Joaquin's dark eyes, which made Santos lean closer with interest.

"How is that?" Santos asked, loathing that he wished to know more. Joaquin snorted and sat back, folding his arms over his filthy work shirt, caked in dirt from the day's chores.

"Father was once promised to marry an English lady from a wealthy house in Cambridge," Joaquin explained, and Santos laughed in disbelief. As he suspected, his brother was spinning yarns to taunt him.

"He was not." His father had no standing to speak of, no attraction to a woman of high status. Why, even with his dashing, dark looks, he could not hope to marry any such lady.

"He was," Joaquin insisted, glaring. He did not hide his irritation at being contradicted. "It was many years ago, and his betrothed chose to marry another."

Santos could see his brother truly believed the words he spoke, but how? How could he when they stood in their leaky cottage, sunburned and hungry, without a guinea to their names?

"Why would any lady opt to wed Father? He has nothing to offer," Santos protested without a modicum of tact. He did not fear a lashing from his father and, despite the ludicrous tale, Santos could not help but be intrigued. Joaquin seemed to debate whether to elaborate on the story, but what he saw in Santos's eyes seemed to encourage him onward. With a deep sigh, he continued to reiterate what he knew.

"At one time, Father's family was well-off. They befell a terrible scandal and lost their fortune, causing them all to become outcasts of society. That is why we live in these rural parts of the country. We cannot return to Barcelona, lest we are shamed."

Santos tried to make sense of what he was being told. Some of the tales did make sense to his young mind. His father had always spoken properly and had insisted his sons do the same. He refused to take them to the cities or to the market, regardless of how much Santos begged. Why, if not to shield them from possible ridicule?

Moreover, Rafael was a terrible farmer. To say his skill was poor was saying it kindly. He clearly was not the kind of man who had been reared among dairy cows or in peach orchards. Yet, even at his tender age, Santos could not help but feel that his brother did not know the true story in its entirety.

"Why have I never heard of this before?" Santos demanded. "Why would Father have told you but not me?"

Joaquin grunted as though his brother was a foolish child.

"He did not tell me of his past, Santos. I have overheard enough on the matter to understand on my own."

Santos tittered, albeit nervously. He could not deny that the more he considered Joaquin's words, the more they made sense to him.

"You know nothing, but what you have concocted in your imagination," Santos replied with a certain smugness. "You only wish to believe we have noble blood running through our veins."

Joaquin scowled. His eyes narrowed.

"We could have been the children of another woman, basking in the riches of London. Instead, we are impoverished farmers who will never know the life we deserve. It was not only Father who was cheated but us—and you laugh about it."

Santos managed a look of contrition, even though he did not agree with his brother. He did not fault his brother for wanting a better life, though. On occasion, he, too, had imagined what it would be like to live in a manor house with servants to wait on him hand and foot. What child of a poor farmer would not envision such a thing for himself? Just because he dreamed of it did not make it so.

What is the harm in permitting Joaquin's whimsy? he reasoned, never one to cause a fuss. He enjoyed jesting with Joaquin and did not like conflict in the least. He was much like his mother in that regard.

Joaquin could see he was not believed. He rose from his spot in a huff of indignation.

"You may snigger all you wish," Joaquin hissed. "One day, I will find this woman who recanted on her promise to marry Father, and I will see that she answers for her crimes."

Santos lost his boyish grin, the words distressing him deeply.

"What crimes?" Santos demanded. "She did nothing wrong if her family permitted the union she accepted. Surely, she cannot be faulted for such a decision."

"And what of our family?" Joaquin demanded. "We were made to suffer for her change of heart."

Santos's head was beginning to swim at the queer logic. He no longer understood the conversation and longed for his brother to leave him in peace—or at least leave him. It was difficult for him to feel at ease while his father continued to scream at his mother, and Rafael's voice rose with each word he howled.

"You cannot be certain this tale is true," Santos reminded him. "No one has told you that such an event occurred."

Joaquin smirked, his dark eyes flashing.

"You are incorrect, my puerile brother. I know she is real for I know her name."

"Is that a fact?" Santos asked, unable to strike the dubiousness from his lips.

"Yes." Joaquin's eyes gleamed triumphantly. "Her name is Anna."

Santos could not stifle his laughter this time, and he giggled almost hysterically as Joaquin's eyes darkened to a nearly terrifying hue.

"What do you find so amusing?" he demanded.

"Anna?" Santos echoed. "I know tens of Annas here in Corraco. How many might there be in England?"

He did not bother to question how his brother, without an escudo to speak of, would ever hope to cross the ocean to Britain and seek this "Anna" he hoped to confront for such a ridiculous reason.

Perhaps I should not indulge his fancy after all. He is nothing short of mad if he believes any of this.

"I will learn more about her in due time," Joaquin growled, petulant indignation coloring his face. "Perhaps I will go there and promise to marry her daughter before leaving her for another woman!"

Again, Santos emitted peals of laughter. How could Joaquin possibly hope to achieve such a task? Any well-to-do Englishman would spot him straightaway. He could not hope to get within a league of said Anna, let alone win the hand of her daughter. Joaquin had quite enough of being mocked and spun to leave their shared quarters.

"You will see," he promised. "I will find this Anna, and she will pay us retribution in kind."

The door slammed behind him with such finality, it even caused Rafael to pause his diatribe in the next room. A smile immediately slipped from Santos's lips, and he knew his father was about to burst through the door. His amusement had been short lived now that his father's attention had been aroused.

"What is the meaning of this ruckus?" Rafael growled, looking about. Santos darted his eyes down, preparing for a backhanded slap to his slender face.

"Forgive me, Father," he said quickly. "I did not mean to slam the door."

As difficult as Joaquin could be, the boy was still his brother and therefore worthy of Santos's protection. Santos would spare his brother Rafael's wrath. His father's eyes narrowed and Santos waited, but the man only grunted.

"Savages. I raise savages because of your mother." He whirled and stomped from the room, just as his oldest son had moments prior. Santos found himself staring after Rafael, his mind racing as his father's words swam in his head. How many times had he heard that very phrase? Yet, suddenly, it had new meaning.

Could Joaquin be correct? Had Father been heir to a fortune and promised to a wealthy heiress?

Santos pushed the notion out of his mind, knowing that, truth or not, it did not much matter. They could not change the past, and this Anna was certainly not to blame for the downfall of the Conostogas.

Perhaps one day, when I am a man, I will ask Father about this directly, Santos mused. Yet, even as he thought it, he knew he was not apt to do so. Santos was already wise enough at the age of eight to leave well enough alone. If Rafael wished to discuss his past, he would do it without prompting or questioning, and Santos would not push the issue. That was much more Joaquin's way than his.

No, Santos knew he would live a simple life and do as he was expected. He did not seek the adventures that Joaquin seemed determined to find.

Santos did not seek trouble—but that did not mean that trouble did not seek him.

CHAPTER ONE

Antoinette Baxter and Joshua Milner stood together, their heads bowed as though they feared being overheard by passersby. Samuel studied them closely, debating whether to intrude or wait. This was not the first time he had seen the head of housekeeping and the young waiter together, and if he were a suspicious man, he might have regarded the scene with wariness.

Yet his logical and calm demeanor told him that there was no reason for reservation. After all, she was a middle-aged, widowed woman, and he was barely out of childhood. Moreover, if there was a matter between them, Samuel knew it was none of his business. He was not the maître d' of the hotel because of his propensity for gossip, after all. It was his discretion which had elevated him to the position he maintained and proudly kept.

He waited for a moment, knowing that the guest he represented stood impatiently at the front desk, demanding his chambers be prepared. At last, the duo parted ways, and Samuel hurried toward Mrs. Baxter for instruction.

Antoinette was a formidable fixture at the Balfour Hotel. She had been there longer than anyone could remember, a fixture in the luxury establishment. She oozed propriety and stability, her graying hair piled upon her stern face, as though the strands feared movement without reprisal.

Although her uniform was customarily black to represent her standing among the white and ebony–clad servants, Samuel truly could not envision her in any other color. Colors, he imagined, were terrified of her tall stature and often pinched face.

"Mrs. Baxter," Samuel called. "Lord Garrison has arrived and he is quite irate that his chambers are not prepared. What shall I tell him?"

Antoinette cast him a look of exasperation as though he were responsible for the setback. Samuel could not help but wither beneath her stare although he knew he had no fault in this particular mishap.

"What has Cora been doing all morrow if not preparing the third-floor quarters?" she demanded. Samuel had no response for such a query. The chambermaids were not instructed under his watch, but he felt a flush of shame all the same. He marveled at her ability to induce such a reaction from him.

"I could not say, Mrs. Baxter."

"Never you mind," Antoinette sighed, gathering her simple skirt to hurry toward the stairs. "I will tend to Cora. Explain to Lord Garrison that his chambers will be ready forthwith."

Samuel pitied poor Cora as he moved to oblige the housekeeper's instructions, but he was grateful that he was no longer under Antoinette's penetrating stare. There would undoubtedly be a breeze when Antoinette set her sights upon Cora, and he was secretly pleased he would not bear witness to the tirade.

Lord Garrison huffed rudely when he saw Samuel.

"I have waited quite long enough!" he growled. "When will my quarters be ready?"

Lord Garrison was a bracket-faced, beetle-browed man, hard on the eyes and with the foul disposition to match. He was also a long-time guest of the hotel and, as Samuel well knew, must be treated with the utmost respect.

Matthew looked away in embarrassment, pretending to busy himself with the log book, and Samuel paid little mind to the receptionist. Careful to avoid Lord Garrison's porcine eyes, he bowed humbly.

"I am told you will be escorted up forthwith, my lord."

"This is preposterous!" the man cried with far more agitation than the situation warranted. "Where is Charlton Balfour? I am a distinguished guest! I am—"

"You are obnoxiously loud," a voice interjected, and Samuel's eyes darted toward it as the Duke of Holden entered the lobby. "My word, Garrison, what on God's earth is causing your apoplexy?"

Lord Garrison balked as James neared, his lovely wife, Lydia, on his arm. Samuel felt a swell of affection when he saw the duchess. He was particularly fond of Lydia. Her husband was quite another matter, but Samuel again knew his place was not to judge the relationships of the upperclassmen.

"Your Grace!" Lord Garrison cried. "I-I had not expected to see you!"

"Would it have sweetened your sourness if you had?" James asked wryly, turning his attention to Samuel. "Good morrow, Samuel."

"Your Grace." Samuel bowed and shifted his eyes toward the duchess. "Your Grace."

Samuel was just as surprised by the arrival of Lady Elizabeth's brother and sister-in-law. He had not been aware that they were due for a visit. He was pleased to see Lydia. He regarded her as a friend, despite the vast difference in their status, but he did not wish to rouse her husband's unfounded jealousies yet again.

I will keep my distance, he vowed, but he reasoned that he might not need to work tirelessly at such a feat. The duchess seemed peaked in her condition, the child she carried due at any time.

"Lord Garrison!" Antoinette called, gliding down the stairs seamlessly. "Do forgive the terrible wait. We were forced to remove a guest, and it was rather unpleasant I fear."

Samuel gaped at the blatant lie, but the housekeeper's fib only seemed to please the crotchety lord.

"Is that a fact?" he murmured as Antoinette snapped at a nearby bellboy.

"Indeed," she continued, deliberately avoiding Samuel's gaze. "Did Mr. Cassidy not explain? Never mind. Your chambers are prepared, and I have instructed Cora to have a bath drawn for you. This way, if you please."

Antoinette turned back around, and Samuel was again struck by her efficiency. She always seemed to know precisely what to say in any situation.

"She is quite a character, is she not?" the duke chuckled as Antoinette disappeared with Lord Garrison. "She will be difficult to replace when she retires."

Samuel swallowed a smile. Antoinette Baxter would work until her very dying day, he was certain. His only hope was that he was not the one to find her body when that day came.

"Forgive me, Your Graces, I was unaware of your arrival," Samuel confessed, feeling foolish to say it. "Shall I inform Lady Elizabeth and the dowager duchess of your presence?"

Samuel was distracted by the protrusion at the duchess's belly, and he wondered if there was a matter with the child she carried. The thought troubled him, but he could not fathom another reason for them to appear without notice. Not that Samuel would ever be so brazen as to ask. He quickly darted his dark eyes back toward the duke, who shook his head in response to Samuel's question.

"There is no need to upend anyone from their business. I am quite sure my sister has her hands full with young James and my mother is bonding with..."

The duke's voice seemed to catch then and Lydia cast her husband a warning look, which Samuel did not claim to understand.

"...with Mrs. Balfour," he concluded, the words spilling from his mouth in a much deeper tone. "However, I would very much enjoy a bedchamber. The duchess could use a rest."

"Of course, Your Grace."

Samuel turned to Matthew, who had already found a suite for the unexpected pair on the fifth floor where all the family resided.

"Daniel," Samuel called, clapping his hands to call upon a bellboy lingering nearby awaiting instruction. "Retrieve the duke's items from their coach and see them upstairs."

"At once, Mr. Cassidy."

James paused and cast Samuel a sheepish look through a peripheral gaze.

"I never did have an opportunity to thank you for your kindness when we were here in the wintertime."

The statement was unexpected but Samuel did not permit his surprise to show on his face.

"I haven't any clue what you mean, Your Grace. I am a servant. It is my job to ensure you and yours are well cared for under my watch."

James opened his mouth to reply, but Lydia tugged on his arm.

"Come along, darling," she urged. "I do need my rest."

As they glided away, Lydia peered over her shoulder with a warm smile for Samuel, and he bowed his head humbly. He was pleased to know that she had not forgotten him either. Theirs was not an affair of the heart but rather a friendship that had been borne from mutual understanding. Samuel had no interest in disrupting a marriage, least of all one between a duke and his wife.

"Quite a morning thus far," Matthew commented, exhaling as though he had endured the brunt of it. "I do hope this is not how the day intends to go."

"You will endure," Samuel chuckled wryly. "We should be grateful that there is not a gala for which to prepare."

"My word, you should not say such things," Matthew muttered. "Next we know, Mr. Balfour will burst forth from the office with a list of guests to be sent invitations."

Samuel chuckled, but he knew Matthew was not being fantastical. They had certainly prepared parties with little notice in the past.

"Indeed," he agreed. "I should not jinx us in this matter."

But it seemed that Samuel no longer held Matthew's attention. The concierge's eyes were trained on the entryway at his back. Samuel turned, not quite comprehending the expression on Matthew's face. He was sure he had never seen quite as profound a look of awe.

"My word," Matthew breathed, echoing Samuel's very thoughts when his dark eyes rested upon the figure who glided toward them. The lady was quite a sight to behold.

Samuel was not a man of sheltered upbringing. He had seen far more than most at the age of nine and twenty, but never had his eyes befallen a comelier article than the woman who moved toward them, her face prim and unsmiling. The lack of geniality upon her visage did nothing to discount from her fine features and brilliant cobalt eyes.

"I would like a room," she said crisply and without preamble. Samuel found his breath catching as he took in the cream of her honey-kissed complexion, a fine chin cinched with the bow of her broad-brimmed bonnet.

She was not quite dressed well enough to be a noblewoman but her attire dictated that she was bred among wealth, nonetheless. Her dark blue eyes fell on him and a slight frown formed at her brow.

"Is there a matter?" she asked haughtily, throwing her head back to peer directly into Samuel's face. "Or do you go about gawking at all your guests?"

Samuel's face flushed with humiliation, and his jaw twitched slightly at her brusque manner. She might have the face of an angel, but she spoke like a shrew. Although, he could not deny that he felt a peculiar sensation of warmth around her despite the chill she seemed to attempt to expel.

"Forgive me, madam," he said stiffly, turning away. He did not miss Matthew's sympathetic gaze as he made his way out of the lobby.

"Have you a reservation, madam?" Samuel heard the concierge ask.

"Must I have one? It is September, is it not? I would not think it would be difficult to find a bedchamber in the autumn."

Samuel ducked around the corner, something stopping him from returning to his duties. Oddly, he found himself relieved that he was not the only one she was rude to. It seemed to be her way.

It was more than her comely face and short manner that intrigued Samuel. She seemed to be unaccompanied. There was not another soul in sight. He was sure he had never seen such a sight.

Who is she? Why has she come here without an escort?

He reasoned, of course, that she might have a handmaid or cousin in a waiting coach, but that would be highly unusual. Why had they not joined her?

"You need not have a reservation," Matthew assured her. "Your name will suffice."

"Lorna Hastings," she replied without hesitation but Samuel could not help but feel she was being untruthful. His travels had indeed taught him many things—to follow his well-honed instincts was one of them.

"Mrs. Hastings, I have a lovely bedchamber on the second floor. Shall I have the bellhop—"

"The second floor?" she interjected. "That is the least luxurious, is it not?"

Matthew clearly bristled at the question, but he was far too composed to lose his temper with a guest—no matter how incorrigible she might be. To Matthew's credit, however, he did not permit the slight to go unattested.

"Madam, this is the Balfour Hotel. There is not a floor nor chamber which is less than pristine, I assure you."

"Prove it," she shot back, and Samuel almost gasped aloud.

My word!

"Pardon me?" Matthew choked, his tone echoing Samuel's very thoughts.

"Prove it to me. I wish to see a suite on every floor. I do not believe that they are all equal. In fact, I believe the second floor is closer to the servants' quarters and therefore rife with rats."

Matthew balked at the mere mention of vermin inside the hotel, and Samuel was unsure if he was aghast or awed by Mrs. Hastings and her liberal mouth.

Moreover, she was right—not about the rats, of course, but that the second floor was used for the guests with less means and prestige.

How did she know? Has she been here before?

"Which floor would you prefer, Mrs. Hastings?" Matthew asked through clenched teeth. Samuel could see it was taking a great deal for him to maintain his composure. First Lord Garrison, now this queer woman and her demands.

Perhaps Matthew is correct—the day may go terribly after all.

"It is *Miss* Hastings," she corrected him. "And I would prefer the fifth floor, but I know you will not permit it unless I marry into this family somehow. Seeing as Xavier Balfour has married a duke's daughter and Charlton Balfour remains wed to his reclusive wife, I imagine I shall see myself content with quarters on the fourth floor."

A peculiar feeling of unease touched Samuel's gut, and he slowly stepped out of the shadows, hoping to catch Matthew's eye. The concierge was far too flustered to look up, but Samuel did not step back. He felt that the receptionist might need solidarity in this matter for there was something underlying in Miss Hastings' words that indicated trouble.

She does seem to know a great deal about the comings and goings of the Balfours, Samuel thought, a flash of protectiveness sweeping through him. *What brings her here?*

The bellhops had not yet returned to the lobby, and Matthew reluctantly ambled around the side of the counter as Miss Hastings pressed the chamber key into her purse.

"Shall I fetch your trunks, Miss Hastings?" Matthew asked, but Samuel stepped forward at once.

"I will get them, Matthew," he said, eager to learn more about this curt but mysterious woman.

"My items will arrive later his afternoon," she replied without looking back. She sailed up the winding staircase, leaving the two men to, once again, stare at her dubiously. She did not pause to see if she was being followed, almost as though she hoped she was not.

Is she running away from us? The notion was absurd.

"Has she been here before, Matthew?" Samuel asked and the younger man shook his head slowly.

"I daresay, I would remember having seen her," he muttered. "Yet she does seem to know a great deal about the hotel, does she not?"

Matthew moved forward, realizing that Miss Hastings had fallen out of view, but Samuel remained in his place, his mind whirling. He was somewhat relieved to note that Matthew had taken exception to Miss Hastings comments about the Balfours and their marriages.

What a queer woman, Samuel thought, willing himself to look away. There was much work to be done and he could not stand about, considering the private matters of the guests. Whoever Miss Lorna Hastings was, she had nothing to do with him. He was just a mere servant, after all. Samuel did not need to call attention to himself by questioning the guests.

I am the last person who has any right to stick my nose in the affairs of anyone, he mused. *How would I feel to know that someone was watching me?*

The idea made him shudder, and he hurried off to the dining room to oversee the waiters preparing lunch service.

CHAPTER TWO

The concierge remained in the doorway, looking uncomfortable as she walked about the quarters with skeptical eyes.

"You are certain this is the best you have?" she demanded, her nose wrinkling with mild disgust. Inwardly, her heart nearly burst with excitement. In her most vivid imagination, she had never foreseen such opulence.

"Miss Hastings, you did demand this floor, which, as you pointed out, is reserved for the highest nobility. Have you a title of which I am unaware?"

She spun and glared at him, noting his skepticism, but her pulse was racing wildly.

You must be cautious, she warned herself.

"This will do," she retorted, removing her gloves to toss them aside and waving Matthew away dismissively.

"Is there anything else I can do for you, Miss Hastings? Have you an escort joining you? Shall I send for an abigail?"

"This will suffice," she said again, maintaining a note of arrogance into her tone. "Was I unclear?"

Matthew's mouth became a fine line, but he bowed stiffly.

"As you wish, miss."

He seemed both relieved and reluctant to leave her, not that she could blame him.

I went too far with this, she realized. *I should not have made such a production in my attempt to appear authentic.*

She paused to exhale, forgetting that she held so dearly to a breath, but now that she found herself alone, she knew she could gather her thoughts and continue with her quest.

She gazed at her reflection in the glass, noting the translucency of her skin. She hoped that the servants had not taken note of her pale complexion.

They are servants, she reminded herself. *They are not to note anything. They are to address the whims of the guests, nothing more, and disappear back behind the tapestry as though they are furniture. I need not worry about them.*

Yet she already knew the Balfour Hotel was not akin to other households. The servants were not only staff but men and women who had sometimes been born and bred on the property. From what she had learned, Emmeline Compton, the owner's daughter, had maintained personal relationships with the staff, much to the chagrin of her father and brother.

I must proceed less conspicuously, she thought, already regretting the way she had burst through the doors with so much flair.

She was not a fool. Her dress, while the best she could afford, was hardly on par with the elegant silks she longed to own for this purpose. Still, she knew her face was lovely enough to overcome passing suspicions.

I must mind my tongue forthwith.

Before traveling to Luton, Lorna had devised a scheme that had seemed flawless. She would fashion her best clothes, gather the remainder of her money, and portray herself as an affluent member of society as to secure quarters in the renowned Balfour Hotel. As her dealings with the highest echelons of society were fleeting, she had been forced to muster the slim recollections of the ladies she had encountered in her one and twenty years. From the recesses of her mind, she adopted their mannerisms, mimicked their dress, and attempted to speak as best she could with her limited experience.

Yet now, she was concerned she had been too forceful with her haughtiness. Certainly, the two servants she had met seemed to regard her with skepticism and not as the graceful lady she was attempting to portray.

You will not be here long, she reminded herself. *You haven't the means nor the time to extend this stay beyond a few days.*

She hoped it would be enough.

It will need to be. Otherwise, I will return to Cambridge destitute, and this journey would have been for naught.

Inhaling a deep breath, she fumbled to remove the bonnet from her classically beautiful face, allowing for a cascade of dark hair to fall around the ruffles of her swelling neckline.

Perhaps she had not thought this entirely through.

In her mind's eye, she saw the tall, dark maître d' eyeing her from where he thought he was unobserved in the shadows. She recalled how he and the receptionist had bowed heads to speak of her as she ascended the stairs.

Befriend them. Make them your ally, not your enemy. They are the best way for you to learn the truth you seek.

She had been warned about the deep-seated and carefully guarded secrets of the Balfour Hotel, but that was why she was there—to learn them all, particularly the ones pertaining to her.

A gentle knock on the door startled her, and with a hand on her chest, she called out, "Enter."

To her surprise, a dashingly handsome man appeared, smartly dressed and smiling curiously as he lingered at the threshold.

"Forgive the intrusion, Miss Hastings. I am Xavier Balfour," he explained. "I wished to welcome you to the Balfour Hotel personally."

She did not allow it to show outwardly, but inside, her heart was thumping furiously. She knew Xavier's appearance had little to do with welcoming and all to do with learning who she was and from where she hailed.

The servants have already called upon him, ringing the alarm of suspicion. Do not tell me this is over before it has even begun.

"Charmed, Mr. Balfour," she replied, extending her hand for him to take. He seemed slightly shocked as he approached her carefully, the shadow in his green eyes darkening. Uncomfortably, he accepted her hand and bowed politely, and it was only then that she realized her hand was bare.

Quickly, she withdrew her palm and spun away as if Xavier's presence had suddenly become an inconvenience.

"Is this your first visit to Luton?" Xavier asked, and she felt her neck stiffen. It was clear that the younger male Balfour was not prone to tact. Yet she had been forewarned of that also.

Tread carefully, she warned herself. *You must not antagonize him.*

"It is not," she replied but offered little else.

"Do forgive me if I am mistaken, Miss Hastings, but you have not been a guest here before."

"Is that a query?" she demanded, whirling back about, her skirts swirling with the same annoyance she displayed upon her face. To her dismay, Xavier met her eyes unflinchingly.

"Indeed, it was. Have you been a guest here in the past?" His directness was somewhat unnerving, but she did not falter.

He is not a servant. He will not be smarted by firm words. I must treat him with more decorum. He was once infamous for his affection for women. Perhaps I can use that to my advantage.

She forced a becoming smile upon her face and cocked her head upward coquettishly, blinking her eyes.

"Would you not remember me if I had?" she offered. If possible, Xavier's expression grew even darker, and she realized she had made yet another mistake.

Banter will not work. He is no longer the Lothario he once was, not since his marriage to Elizabeth Burney. I will not get anywhere this way.

Insofar, her plan was unraveling terribly. She had barely been in Luton an hour and she was ready to leave without learning a thing.

"Have you no companion with you?" Xavier continued, his dubiousness filling the room as his eyebrows raised higher.

"I have not."

"Then perhaps I should send an abigail to assist you? I should not need to tell you how...improper it is that you have come to the hotel without an escort."

She balked at the idea. She could not think of a worse fate than having a servant following her about for her stay.

"I would prefer to be left in peace, else I would have brought a companion," she replied quickly. It was not the response he had expected.

"Is that a fact?" Xavier asked with some skepticism, and she found herself becoming genuinely irate by the questions.

"Mr. Balfour, I do appreciate you calling upon me, but I would like to rest now. I have had a long journey."

"From where?" he challenged.

"Wales," she said quickly. His eyes narrowed further as he considered her answer.

"What was your business there? Surely, you do not hail from Wales."

While she had known her presence would certainly cause a fuss, she had not anticipated being questioned so quickly upon her arrival. She simply was not prepared for the endless queries with which Xavier pelted her.

"That is a matter of a personal nature," she said crisply.

"Please," she insisted before he could speak again. "If there is nothing else..."

He parted his lips to respond but seemed to reconsider his words. Slowly, a spark lit his eyes, and she loathed to hear what he might say next.

"I hope you will join my family for supper this evening," he offered, and the words took her aback.

No! A small voice cried out worriedly in her head, but she dismissed it instantly.

"I would be honored," she replied demurely. "Thank you, Mr. Balfour."

He nodded curtly, smiling tightly and bowed again.

"Miss Hastings," he said. He paused at the doorway and turned back to study her face carefully before speaking.

"The Balfour Hotel is a household of prestige and decorum. We pride ourselves on our discretion."

"I am pleased to hear that," Lorna answered, knowing he had not finished what he intended to say.

"We will do all that is required to uphold the reputation of this hotel," he continued as if she had not spoken. Lorna was unsure how to respond and therefore did not, and instead maintained her soft smile upon her lips.

"Rest, Miss Hastings. We will speak again at dinner."

The warning hung over the room well after Xavier had departed, and she swallowed the lump of concern forming in her delicate windpipe. Xavier had been alerted of her arrival by the wary servants, she was certain. There was no other reason he would have come so quickly, not when she had no prior reservation.

You should leave this place, she warned herself, but again she ignored her good sense and faced her reflection in the glass over the toilet once more.

"You will not leave," she said aloud, squaring her slouching shoulders. "You are Lorna Hastings, daughter of a wealthy merchant. You are in Luton on behalf of your father, seeking new opportunities."

Or that was what she intended to tell the Balfours when questioned. The tale sounded hollow to her own ears, but it was far too late to create another story. She was already in the purview of everyone she had encountered thus far.

All will be well. Keep to your story and no one will be the wiser. There is a real merchant named Henry Hastings, and he does have a daughter by the name of Lorna.

She had taken a grave risk coming to the hotel as Lorna Hastings, assuming that the merchant's daughter had never traveled with him, but from what she had learned, Lorna Hastings was agoraphobic and did not leave their estate in the east of Wales for extended periods of time, if at all.

She could only hope that the Balfours did not know of the Hastings' shameful secret.

Or that they do not question how a woman who is supposed to be one and thirty appears a decade younger.

Ah, there were so many flaws to her scheme, but what choice did she have but to oversee her intentions? If she did not, she would be worse off than when she started—her purse empty and without a place to go. She met her own gaze in the glass again and firmed her mouth.

"You are Lorna Hastings, daughter of Henry Hastings. You are in Luton on behalf of your father, seeking new opportunities."

She wondered how many times she would need to say the words before they sounded truthful, but she realized that they never would quite sound right. How could they when she was not the woman she was pretending to be?

With a sigh, she turned back toward the majestic canopied bed, which was bigger than any she had ever seen in her existence. Where would she have such an occasion to see such an extravagance. Despite her brusque entrance, she had been awed by what she had seen in the Balfour Hotel.

There was yet another knock at her door, and she expected that Xavier had returned with another warning, but to her surprise, it was the maître d' she had seen in the lobby when she had first arrived.

"Your trunk has arrived, Miss Hastings," he explained, lugging in the badly worn piece. It looked terribly out of place amidst the splendid surroundings, and her face flushed with humiliation.

Had he seen the driver who had left the trunk? Her head grew dizzy at the idea.

He told me he would arrive at midday so I could meet him privately! Why has he come so early?

She decided to ask if the delivery had been witnessed.

"No, miss," he replied, but she could not help but feel apprehensive. "The trunk was left with a note on the steps outside, indicating that it was to be delivered to your rooms. Is there a matter? Are these not your items?"

"They are," she replied quickly. "I had wished to have a word with the driver was all. You are dismissed..."

She found herself casting him a furtive look through the side of her long lashes. She had not noticed how dashing was the man, with dark eyes and thick black hair. There was something foreign in appearance about him, yet his English was flawless. Certainly, the Balfours would not employ foreigners, after all.

That would be beneath them, Lorna thought with some bitterness. *Their servants must be of the highest caliber.*

Idly, she wondered if a person such as herself would even be hired to clean chamber pots in there or if her lineage was simply too poor.

"Yes, Miss Hastings." The maître d' turned to leave, but before he reached the door, she called out to him.

"I would like a pot of tea," she told him. "Is this something you could arrange?"

He seemed stunned by the question and nodded quickly.

"Of course, Miss Hastings. I am at your disposal for anything you might require."

Her eyes narrowed slightly as she turned to stare at him fully but she noted he kept his eyes properly averted.

Why, then, did she feel as though he could see right through her?

Nonsense, she chided herself. *You are being paranoid.*

"Then see to it," she told him, waving her hand again. "Do be quick about it."

"Yes, Miss Hastings." He paused just as Xavier Balfour had and cast her another cautious look. "I am Samuel."

Samuel. The unsolicited introduction filled her with an unexpected shiver of delight although why, she could not say. The feeling was unsettling. She could not allow such things and, she quickly masked her attraction the maître d', Samuel, with curtness.

"Run along then, Samuel," she muttered, turning her face so that he might not see the blush forming on her cheeks. When he departed, she hurried to sit on the chaise, fanning herself with her bare hand. Her temperature had risen to an unexpectedly feverish level.

Enough now, Nora. Keep your wits about you and begin your investigation, for if you fail at this, you will never get another opportunity. Lord only knows what the Balfours are capable of when their reputation is threatened.

She shuddered at the thought.

CHAPTER THREE

Matthew had returned to the front desk when Samuel made his way into the lobby after delivering Lorna Hastings' trunk. The concierge had not been there when the baggage had arrived, leaving Samuel to chance upon the dilapidated box alone. He found himself somewhat relieved that he was the one to have found it. There was little mistaking that the careworn trunk did not belong to that of an upper-classman, regardless of the airs Lorna Hastings presented.

Its arrival had further enhanced the deep suspicion Samuel was feeling, despite reminding himself that he was not to involve himself in the affairs of the beautiful woman, not matter how strong his desire to protect her. Samuel had hurried the trunk up to her suite, without comment to anyone. It was not his business, and he would not make it so by asking unnecessary questions. However, if Miss Hastings wished to share information of her own accord, Samuel would not stop her.

He had learned nothing new, of course, leaving him even more perplexed as he ambled through the lobby. The sound of raised voices caught his attention, and he found himself turning toward the office.

"...Father. I cannot be certain but—"

"Xavier, you must stop with this," Charlton Balfour snapped back at his son before the younger man could complete his thought. "You constantly entertain a suspicious mind. We do not investigate guests unless they give us cause. Matthew, shame on you for bringing such nonsense to our attention."

Samuel paused, feeling slight guilt that he had taken to eavesdropping not once, but twice that morning, but he felt as though the two incidents were closely related.

They are discussing Miss Hastings, he thought with more interest than he knew he deserved.

"Forgive me, Mr. Balfour," Matthew muttered. "I felt that she did not belong on the fourth floor but she insisted. She seems...odd."

"If she has the means to pay, I do not care where a single woman stays. She is hardly a threat to the hotel," Charlton growled. "Why are you interrupting my morning with such nonsense?"

"Father," Xavier pressed urgently. "She is unaccompanied. She hasn't even a handmaid!"

"So, you have invited her to supper tonight. I will question her myself although the name Hastings—I daresay she is the daughter of Henry Hastings."

There was a short silence as the concierge and Xavier processed Charlton's thought in their own minds.

"The merchant?" Xavier asked finally. "Has he a daughter?"

"One, if I recall," Charlton replied. "So, you see? This is simply ridiculous. Now if you will both excuse me, I have more pressing matters to attend this morning than the trite gossip of the hotel staff."

Samuel ducked out of the lobby, knowing he was about to be caught listening to the private conversation. Yet when he turned, he almost jumped clear off the floor in shock.

Lorna Hastings stood watching, her eyes narrowed.

"Do you oft go skulking about the hotel where you are employed?" she demanded. Samuel's jaw tightened. "I imagine that is the best way to learn the secrets, however."

"I was not skulking," he denied. "I was..."

He trailed off, knowing he lacked the disposition for falsehoods. He had been seen listening and there was little he could do to deny it now. Samuel's face flushed. He was grateful for his dark complexion, lest she notice.

"Skulking. Spying perhaps?" Miss Hastings chuckled. There was a near-lilt to her tone that Samuel found utterly charming. Her laughter reminded him of songbirds on a spring morning.

"Hardly," he answered, straightening his back and attempting to shake off the effect the woman had on him. "Is there a matter in which I might assist you, Miss Hastings?"

A coy grin formed around her lips, and Samuel was certain he had never seen such a luscious set of lips. It embarrassed him that he gazed upon her in such a way. Regardless of who she was, she was a guest at the hotel where he worked.

A hauntingly lovely and mysterious guest of this hotel.

"I imagine you have forsaken my request for tea," she replied, and Samuel's mouth parted. He had forgotten, but even as he realized it, he knew that she had not come to the lobby because of his inattention. There had not been enough time for her to realize the tea was not being made. Moreover, there was a bell in her room if she desired a waiter to attend to her. There was little cause for her to have come to the lobby for such a trivial matter.

"I have not, miss. I will have it to you forthwith," Samuel replied slowly, wondering if perhaps he had not caught the comely Miss Hastings in a lie of her own.

"Never mind that now," she said, reaching for his arm. "Come along with me."

His instinct was to pull away from her grasp, but Samuel did not. Shocked by her brazenness, he allowed himself to be pulled aside into a cove where she released him. She stepped much too close to be considered proper, but even so, he did not draw back. Her nearness was tantalizing, and he found himself studying her near-flawless features, knowing he would likely never be so close to her again.

Samuel could not understand what enchantment had come over him when it came to the beautiful Miss Hastings. He felt as though he had fallen under a spell, and he was not sure he wished for it to be lifted.

"I have been invited to supper with the Balfours," she explained, further enhancing Samuel's perplexity. "What must I know?"

Confusion flooded Samuel, and he eyed her without understanding her question. His attention was still focused along the delicate lines of her face, the smooth creaminess of her complexion, the little wrinkle that had appeared between her brows as she scrunched them together in concentration. She was proving to be more complex a personality than Samuel had ever known. One moment, he was certain she was mocking him, the next she appeared to be almost vulnerable.

"Know?" he echoed. "About what?"

Her face twisted into a slight grimace, as she scanned his face. Then, for a moment, she simply searched his eyes, and Samuel was certain he could see the wheels moving about like a heavily cogged machine before she spoke.

"Perhaps I was a tad...rude with you earlier," she offered, and Samuel inhaled sharply. Whoever this woman claimed to be, she was certainly not of high standing. What noblewoman would apologize to a servant, even if she had been uncouth? It was her right to treat the staff in whatever manner she saw fit. Samuel's brow furrowed.

"You were not, Miss Hastings," he muttered, keeping his beliefs to himself. He was trying desperately not to involve himself in the affairs of this woman, but the matter was becoming increasingly difficult when she would not let him beand a part of him was so drawn to her vulnerability.

"I was," she insisted, and Samuel's eyes grew wide with disbelief.

The Balfours will see right through her charade in minutes. Whoever she is, and whatever her farce, she hasn't a clue how to behave as a lady.

"You must stop saying such things," he hissed before he realized his worry had found words. He looked about nervously to assure himself that they would be spotted speaking so intimately. Oddly, he was reminded of Antoinette and Joshua earlier that very morning.

So many secrets in this hotel. Why is it any great shock that the guests have them, too?

"Saying what things?" She seemed genuinely confused by his manner, her deep, lovely eyes boring into him with curiosity and Samuel knew he had said too much.

"Miss Hastings, I must return to my duties. Is there another matter?"

"You did not answer my first matter for tea," she reminded him.

"Nor my second when I asked you for your help with the Balfours. I should not task you with a third. You seem to be beetle-headed enough."

Samuel bit the side of his cheek to suppress a grin, but kept his eyes properly averted from her gaze. He was amused that a woman with such an angelic face could spew such cutting remarks from her lips.

"Very well, miss. I will see to your tea." He spun away but not before he caught the aghast look upon her face.

"Samuel," she snapped. "You must help me."

There was an undeniable apprehension in her voice, and reluctantly, he looked back to her.

"Help you how?" he muttered, again looking about. He had never felt so uncomfortable, which was saying quite a lot considering the experiences he had known. He was confused by this woman, perplexed by the feelings which she evoked from him. Even knowing that she was not who she claimed to be could not completely deter him from her allure. Then, there was also the understanding that she was a guest and therefore meant to be treated with respect. He wished that someone would come along and put an end to his queer struggle.

"I wish to know all you know about the Balfours."

Samuel bristled, his sense of loyalty to the Balfours hardened his face and caused his voice to tighten.

"The Balfours are decent and kind employers," he intoned. "I do not know what more I can tell you."

"How long have you been here, Samuel? Were you the maître d' who replaced Honor Wesley?"

"I...yes," he replied uneasily, once more plagued by the uncertainty that this Miss Hastings knew too much. How could she have known the name of the previous maître d'? Samuel himself had only heard tawdry gossip about the whereabouts of Honor Wesley, a man who had apparently left without warning.

"Certainly, you know there are secrets in this hotel," she pressed, again reaching out to touch his arm. On this occasion, Samuel did pull away, albeit reluctantly, stunned that she had so brazenly touched him a second time.

"I know nothing of the sort," he replied, trying futilely to keep his tone steady and unwavering. "This discussion is quite inappropriate. I do not think that Mr. Xavier would like to know you are discussing the household with the servants."

She visibly paled, and Samuel felt a stab of contrition as he shifted his eyes away.

"You misunderstand me," she muttered. "I only mean to be prepared for this unexpected invitation to supper. I mean no harm."

Samuel did not believe that in the least, but he kept his doubts silent, difficult as it was.

"You will find the Balfours to be genial and warm," he offered, unsure if he spoke the truth to her. Would Mrs. Balfour be a trifle disguised if she were not asleep from the drink? Would the dowager duchess be ill at ease with the arrival of her son who had accused her of such terrible crimes? Would Charlton Balfour unearth some sordid detail about his past troubles? It was impossible to know the timbre of the evening, for it could change so hastily from one night to the next.

"Fine," Lorna mumbled, seeming irate by his vague answers. "I suppose you would rather me be fed to the wolves than assist an unchaperoned woman."

Samuel again stifled a grin. Surely, the woman before him was anything but helpless. Moreover, he would have wagered good money that she had come to Luton unchaperoned by choice—if not by fighting choice.

Lord help the man tasked with marrying this one, Samuel thought, but even as the words entered his mind, he could not deny the pang of jealousy the notion created within him. He willed himself to ignore the unwarranted emotions coursing through him.

I will not involve myself in her mischief. I value my employment and the Balfours far too much for that.

"Good day, Miss Hastings," he said, moving to leave yet again.

"Samuel!" Begrudgingly, he turned back toward her, wishing he had the good sense to simply put distance between them before her raw charms consumed him entirely.

"Miss?"

"You must not tell the Balfours what I have asked," she told him, anxiety creeping into her words. "I mean no harm to anyone."

He stared at her for a long moment. She truly was a vision—an impish, untrustworthy vision.

"Good day," he said again without answering her plea.

"You have quite an interesting accent, Samuel."

He froze in his tracks.

"Pardon me?"

"Your accent—from where do you hail?"

"I have not an accent," he snapped with more harshness than he intended, but he turned to stare at her again, his pulse quickening. Never had anyone said such a thing to him.

"You hide it well," she said quietly. "Yet your features dictate that you have Moor blood."

How could she possibly know? No one has ever detected my heritage before.

With mounting dread, Samuel cast her a deadpan look.

"The Balfours would not employ such a man," he answered flatly.

"No, I do not believe they would," she agreed. "Not if they knew better. Good day, Samuel."

It was she who gathered her skirts and moved away, leaving him to gawk after her. The threat was apparent even if Lorna did not complete her thoughts on the matter. He should be appalled, perhaps even worried. Yet he remained utterly beguiled by her.

"Whatever are you doing, Mr. Cassidy?" Antoinette snapped from behind him, causing Samuel to jump. Would there be no end to these women startling him that day?

Indeed, what am I doing? he thought. His instinct was to find Charlton or Xavier Balfour and recite the conversation at once, but his feet did not point in that direction. They remained rooted in place as the queer encounter danced through his mind, blocking even Antoinette from his line of sight.

"My word, Mr. Cassidy, are you unwell?"

"No," Samuel answered quickly, offering her a smile. "I merely forgot where I was to go next."

Antoinette scowled in disapproval.

"You are still a young man yet," she muttered. "If you are taking leave of your senses already, God help us all!"

With that, she turned away, and Samuel forced himself to focus on his duties. He needed not involve himself in whatever it was Lorna Hastings plotted, regardless of what it meant for the Balfours. She had spoken the truth, after all—the Balfours and their ilk were rife with surreptitious knowledge and history. Samuel was not tasked with keeping the family from prying guests. His job was merely to attend to them without question.

Why, then, did guilt surge through him as he went about his business, tending to the waiters in the dining hall?

I will mind my own self, he insisted, but the thought was inane. It was clear to him that, once again, he had unwittingly become entangled in the Balfours' affairs.

CHAPTER FOUR

It did not take much to feel the tension at the dining table that evening. In fact, one would need be a dunce to ignore it, the unease as thick as lingering cigar smoke.

You must not let them fluster you, Nora, she told herself. *They are the ones with the scandals, not you.*

Yet it was impossible to stop her hands from trembling as a young waiter held out her chair and the men rose to greet her upon arrival.

"Thank you for joining us, Miss Hastings," Charlton Balfour boomed, nodding appreciatively at her. "I am afraid my wife was unable to join us this evening, but do permit me to introduce the rest of my family."

He motioned to the people along the table, gauging peerage with precision and accuracy.

"His Grace, the Duke of Holden and wife, Her Grace, the Duchess. Her Grace, the Dowager Duchess of Holden." Charlton gestured down the table, and Nora attempted to gather as much as she could in such a short introduction, but matters were moving much too quickly for her to keep afloat.

"Charmed," Nora said, curtseying as she waited for the rest. She had not been expecting the duke or his kin to be there, but she reasoned that there would be little issue with them—the duchess was ready to birth her child any moment it seemed. There was no hiding the huge swell of her belly. They would be far too distracted with other matters to concern themselves with a guest.

"You have already become acquainted with my son, Mr. Xavier Balfour, I am told," Charlton continued, taking a breath. "His bride, Lady Elizabeth Balfour. This is my son-in-law, Mr. Elias Compton, and his wife, my daughter, Emmeline."

Nora's head was swimming, but she managed to keep a pleasant smile about her mouth.

"I am honored to be here with you," Nora fibbed as she graciously took her chair. While it was true that she had wanted to meet every member of the family, she had not hoped for such an encounter to occur with so many of them together at one time. Her mind had sought solutions as to how she might avoid the supper, but nothing spoke to her easily. It would be uncouth for her to feign illness, and she knew she was already under scrutiny. And truly, she was peckish. Nora could not recall when she had last eaten.

I must not cause a fuss. One evening will not harm me, she reasoned, her mouth nearly watering at the delicious scents about the dining hall.

"It is our pleasure to have you here," Emmeline offered softly, perhaps sensing Nora's nervousness. "How are you finding your accommodations?"

"Much lovelier than I had expected," Nora replied, and she realized she spoke the truth. She hoped her status—or lack thereof—was not shining through in her words, for she had no gauge to compare the Balfour Hotel with any other. It was her first time inside any such place. Yet as a merchant's daughter, she would be well-traveled.

The Balfour Hotel is renowned all about Europe, she reminded herself, taking comfort in the information of her sources.

"I imagine it is much lovelier than anything you have seen," she heard Xavier mutter, but Lady Elizabeth cast him a stare, which seemed to silence him at once. Suddenly, Nora could not help but feel she had been improperly prepared for the Balfours. The women, in particular.

Emmeline seems kind, gentle. I would not expect that from a hotel heiress.

Her husband, too, seemed mild mannered, but Nora had known that about Elias Compton. He had the patience and disposition of a saint.

Nora's eyes moved discretely about the table, catching the curious but kind smile of Lady Elizabeth, and then her brother, the Duke of Holden, who seemed more fixed on the dowager duchess than his own wife.

All of them seemed pleasant, warm—not at all what Nora had been told.

Your information is outdated, she thought. *They only knew what they had heard after they left the hotel. You cannot be certain of anything you were told now. You must relearn everything you believe you know.*

"What brings you to Luton, Miss Hastings?" the duke asked, reaching for a sip of his wine, perhaps realizing that she was looking at him. Nora instantly grew wary, but she stopped herself from reacting to the question. After all, it was one with merit, proper supper conversation. All day, she had worried that Samuel had gone to the Balfours to tell them what she had said about secrets lingering in the halls of the hotel.

Yet she could see no new suspicion among them, only a family of mildly curious souls who wished to know about the new guest.

"Business," she replied, noting that she had taken a long while to answer. "I am here on business."

Xavier snorted contemptuously.

"Pray tell, what business could you possibly have in—" he stopped speaking, his eyes widening in shock as he seemed to consider what business a young, unaccompanied woman might entertain.

"Are you a crack?" he demanded, and Nora did not know whether to laugh or shout at the terrible insult. Certainly, she knew from where it had come, but to blatantly ask a young lady if she were convenient! Nora was as stunned as the rest of the family, none more so than his wife.

"Xavier!" Lady Elizabeth hissed, her ire unmistakable. "How dare you say something so vile to a guest?"

Xavier had the decency to look away, but he did not apologize. Lady Elizabeth turned her attention to Nora, her eyes apologetic.

"Forgive him. He seems to have forsaken his manners."

"I would rather he had forsaken his tongue!" Charlton growled. "My word, Xavier, for shame."

Nora tried to smile, but it proved more difficult than she thought.

"My father is a merchant," Nora began, her voice quavering if only to her own ears. "I have come at his request to seek out op-opportunities."

Dear Lord above!

She had not meant to sputter, and she could feel Xavier's eyes boring into her as she struggled to regain her composure.

You have recited this dozens upon dozens of times. You must not falter now!

"Aha!" Charlton boomed, startling the entire table when he clapped his open palms unceremoniously down onto the table. "I knew it! You see, Xavy! She is whom I thought!"

"Father," Emmeline muttered. "Do mind your own manners now."

"Do you know my father, Mr. Balfour?" Nora breathed, willing her voice to grow stronger. She had entered her lie in an official capacity now, and she could not falter, not if she intended to see it all through.

"He has stayed here on occasion," Charlton replied. "I am stunned he did not send word you were coming. I daresay, he has never appeared unannounced. Shall we be expecting Henry, then?"

Nora shook her head.

"It was a rather sudden decision," Nora answered crisply. "There would have been no time for the mails to reach you."

"The mails?" All eyes were upon her, and she looked about the table, unsure of what her gaffe had been. Yet she was aware she had certainly made one.

Another one.

"Surely, he would have used a messenger," Elias Compton said quietly, meeting her eyes, and Nora was certain she was about to swoon.

A messenger. Of course. These people do not use the mails.

"What did I say?" Nora asked innocently. "The mails?"

She laughed merrily.

"It is what I call the pages," she explained, and a rush of titters passed over the tables. All were amused but three—Xavier Balfour,

Elias Compton, and now, for reasons she could not understand, the Duke of Holden.

This is getting worse by the passing moment. How could I have ever thought I could do this?

She needed to get up and flee, to run far from the hotel, the plan be damned.

Or I might simply blurt out the truth here and now. Let us see how the table might react.

"I know Henry Hastings quite well," the duke growled, leaning over the table to eye her intensely. "*You* are Lorna Hastings?"

Oh...oh, he knows. I am certain he knows. Has he met Lorna in the past?

She reminded herself that she had been aware of all the risk before arriving in Luton. Over and over she had considered what might happen if her true reason for being there might be uncovered but in the end, Nora had decided that it was well worth the risk if she would learn the truth.

"I am his only daughter," Nora replied, holding her head high. She would cling to her tale until she was led to the barracks for holding if necessary.

"I see," the duke muttered, turning his eyes back toward his plate, a slow tinge touching his cheeks. "I had heard..."

He cleared his throat, and Nora's body began to relax as she realized what he was about to say. His suspicion had to do with what he had heard about Lorna Hastings.

He is aware of the real Lorna Hasting's affliction, she realized, but that was a matter with which she could contend. It meant that the Balfours had never laid eyes upon the real Lorna Hastings and that gave Nora great comfort. She was safe...for the time.

"You heard I was a terrible recluse?" she offered brashly. Lady Elizabeth gasped at the frankness of her words.

"I do not believe the duke meant anything so crude, Miss Hastings!" she protested, her face pale as fresh snow. Nora could almost read the thoughts in her head.

My husband calls her a courtesan and my brother, a liar!

"Forgive me, Miss Hastings," the duke mumbled, seeming hauntingly embarrassed. "I meant nothing by it."

"You need not balk, Your Grace. You are quite right—I spent many years afraid to leave the confines of my home. But as you can see, I am pleased to be here, surrounded by good, decent people."

She smiled becomingly and the tension about them seemed to lift slightly, even if Xavier continued to sulk angrily in disbelief.

"If you will forgive me for saying so, Miss Hastings, you do appear a great deal younger than I expected," Charlton offered, but it was yet another matter for which Nora was prepared.

"Perhaps it was all those terrible years spent inside that kept me from aging," she replied lightly. "I did not ruin my skin in the sunlight."

There was a soft, appreciative chuckle around the table, but Nora could see that Xavier was not moved by her explanation.

Perhaps that is because he has the most to hide, she reasoned, fixing her eyes upon him steadfastly. She would not relent because of one soul. The others were warming to her—she was certain.

"We are pleased to have you also," Emmeline said, returning her beam. Nora found herself dissolving some of her reservations until Elias Compton spoke again.

"You seem oddly familiar to me, Miss Hastings," he said, and Nora's back tensed to the point of snapping. It was a dizzying experience, being with this lot. One moment Nora was certain she had overcome, the next, she felt as though she were drowning in the Thames.

He could not remember me after all these years, could he? It seemed highly unlikely. She had not seen Elias since she was almost a child and only then, on passing occasion.

"Do I?" she replied sweetly.

"Indeed," he muttered. A trickle of sweat formed over Nora's brow, and she found herself looking about for means of escape. In her worst thoughts, she never imagined that Elias Compton would be the one to cause her the most concern.

"Forgive me, Mr. Balfour." Nora looked up and saw Samuel standing at her side. It was strangely comforting to have him there, even though he had made his sentiments towards her clear earlier. Still, Nora could not help but feel as though he was her only ally in the hotel.

"What is it, Samuel?" Charlton asked, sitting back in his chair to peer at the maître d'.

"There is a messenger for Miss Hastings."

No one was more confused by the words than Nora, who gazed at the maître d'. Samuel, however, did not meet her eyes.

"Do I?" she murmured.

"Yes, miss. He has asked to speak only with you. He will not speak with another."

"At this hour?" Xavier muttered, seeming unconvinced that any such messenger existed. "How queer."

"Excuse me," Nora said, rising, and the men quickly moved to stand also. "Perhaps it is word from my father."

"Perhaps," Elias agreed, and she did not miss the dubiousness in his word. She turned to follow Samuel from the dining room, her heart thudding tirelessly in her chest. Who could possibly be sending her a messenger? Certainly, no one she knew could afford such an extravagance, and Nora did not have the means to pay any such boy on sight. The sweat that had started against her forehead threatened to slip along her fair cheeks, and suddenly, Nora was finding it very difficult to breathe.

Yet when they retreated to the lobby, only the night concierge, an elderly man by the name of Byron sat. There was not another soul in sight.

"Where is this messenger?" she asked, her eyes darting about.

"This way, miss."

Samuel continued through the lobby and toward the ballroom. More bewilderment seized Nora, and she wondered if she was walking into a perilous scenario.

"Are you quite sure?" she questioned, stopping between the rooms and peering at Samuel with disconcerted eyes.

"Quite," he replied without pausing. She realized that she could either turn back and return to the inquisitive Balfours and their ilk or follow Samuel further into the hotel.

She chose Samuel. Gathering her dress, she hurried after him as he disappeared through the back exit of the ballroom onto the terrace.

Why would a messenger be on the terrace?

There was only one way to know for certain, and with a deep breath, Nora moved across the well-polished floor of the dark chamber until she, too, stood on the veranda where Samuel had finally stopped.

He was alone.

"What is the meaning of this?" Nora's face flushed with anxiety. She could not suppress the lingering nervousness and fear. Was this Samuel's retaliation for her bold words earlier?

"Would you prefer to be at that table?" he asked, turning to face her fully. Nora did not know what to say.

"I-I do not understand," she finally sputtered honestly. "Is there not a messenger?"

"Of course not," Samuel muttered. "You know fully that you are not whom you claim to be. Who would send you word through a page? The king?"

She ignored his sardonic words and stared at him uncomprehendingly.

"I-I do not know what you mean. I am Nora Hastings—" she abruptly stopped when she realized what she said. She begged for apoplexy at that moment, anything to take her away from the hole she continued to dig for herself.

Samuel's face twisted, and Nora attempted to recant her words, but she was far too flustered, knowing that her poor disguise had already been ruined.

"*Nora* Hastings?" he echoed. "Who are you truly?"

"You heard incorrectly!" she insisted. "I said Lorna Hastings."

"You did not!" Samuel snapped. "You need not lie any longer. I have been suspicious of you since the moment you arrived, and now I have good cause."

"You are mad," she huffed, spinning around to leave. "I need not hear this."

"If you do not tell me why you have come here and why you are lying to the Balfours, I will tell them of your deception."

"You will do nothing of the sort!" she retorted, pivoting to glare at him. "Or *I* will tell them of *yours*!"

"I have deceived no one," he growled but even as he spoke, Nora could see the shadow cross over his eyes.

I was correct! He does hide who he is, too!

"You have," she exclaimed ruefully. She had no wish to hurt this man who had just come to her rescue, yet she felt a bit like a caged animal at the moment. "I hear it in your accent. You are a foreigner."

"Lower your voice at once!" he snapped. "You know nothing about me."

"Nor do you of me," she retorted. "I will not stand here and be judged by a servant!"

"You may look down your nose at me, *Miss Hastings*," he snarled. "But your threadbare trunks tell a story you must not want heard. Henry Hastings is a wealthy merchant. He would not permit his daughter to be seen with such ragged baggage. You are no more an upperclassman than I."

Nora opened her mouth to protest his observation, but she knew her arguments were in vain. She had unwittingly let her cover slip, and now Samuel knew about her. Would this mean ruination for her?

I truly was not prepared for this.

Without a word, she spun to run off, but Samuel's strong hand seized her arm and she found herself staring into his dark eyes once more.

"You will tell me who you are," he insisted. "Or I will march you back to the dining hall, and you can explain yourself before the already suspicious men who wait for you."

"They are not suspicious..." she fumbled to say, even though she knew his words were correct. If Samuel did as he threatened, she would not be able to talk her way out of it again.

"They are. Why do you think I made up this laughable excuse and drew you away from them?"

Her eyes narrowed, partially in confusion but mostly in awe. She was nonplussed by the encounter. Was Samuel her friend or foe?

"You brought me here to give me reprieve?" she asked slowly, reluctant to believe him.

"I brought you here hoping you had the good sense to tell me the truth, therefore saving me from turning you in."

"What of your loyalty to the Balfours?" she wondered, unsure if she could trust him. She looked at his hand still encircling her arm. He did not release her, and Nora's eyes traveled up toward his penetrating gaze.

"You went through a great deal of trouble to come here. You are not a woman with means. Have you come here to steal from the Balfours?"

Her face twisted in shock.

"Goodness, no!" she gasped, aghast at the question. "Just because I am not wealthy does not mean I break the commandments!"

His face softened, and he released her arm.

"You obey the commandments," he murmured, almost inaudibly.

"I believe in God's message, of course," she retorted sincerely. Samuel seemed to realize the conversation had taken a twist and moved his thoughts back in the proper direction.

"Then, why? Why have you done this if not for uncouth reasons?"

Nora looked at the ground and blushed.

"I am looking for my father," she replied quietly.

"Your father?" he echoed. "Who might that be?"

Nora inhaled deeply, her eyes lowered in shame.

"I am unsure," she replied quickly. "My mother passed two years ago, and she told me that the man I had always believed was my father was not."

Nora wondered why she was speaking so freely to this skeptical stranger, knowing that all she said could haunt her later. Yet she could not suppress the idea that Samuel could be trusted. Was it the way he looked at her, with tenderness and an underlying protectiveness?

"What makes you think he is here?" Samuel insisted. "And who are you truly?"

"My name is Nora Chalmers," she sighed. "And I have reason to believe that my father is Charlton Balfour."

CHAPTER FIVE

Samuel was unable to sleep that night and rightfully so. The cannon that Nora had fired was both nonsensical and disturbing, but he was unsure what to believe.

Over and over he told himself that he could not permit himself to be part of whatever it was Nora Chalmers hoped to accomplish. He was torn between his loyalty to the Balfours and wanting to help the beautiful, mysterious young woman.

Yet Samuel reminded himself he had much to lose by doing the latter. Nora had not been incorrect—he was not whom the Balfours believed him to be.

The circumstances of my arrival are much different than hers, he protested as though his own mind fought with him. *I have not come here to disrupt the order of the hotel. On the contrary, in fact. I came here to ensure order.*

But had Nora come to wreak havoc upon the very household he had grown to love? They had not spoken a great deal more on the matter at hand, their covert interview interrupted by the surprise arrival of Joshua, who stumbled upon them on the terrace. Samuel had not been concerned that the young lad would speak of what he had seen—a guest and servant in an intimate discussion. Yet being seen had done nothing but add to Samuel's unease.

He knew he would have to speak with Nora again, but he also realized that discretion was paramount.

Samuel was distracted as he dressed for his shift. There was much to process about what Nora had claimed. If she was indeed the daughter of Charlton Balfour, it would mean certain scandal for the hotel. The young lady was no more than one and twenty, if Samuel were to guess, and Charlton Balfour had been married to Anne for a quarter century at least. Lord knew, the Balfours had been the center of enough rumor and innuendo in the past years, starting with the arrival of Elias Compton. Could the hotel withstand another setback? Samuel could not imagine it would.

And then what would become of the Balfours? This hotel is their legacy!

Perhaps Xavier and Lady Elizabeth would fare well, the Duke of Holden likely to take them in, but the others?

He shuddered to consider what such a sordid secret might do to the family, even if it did not lead to financial ruin.

A gentle knock at his door caused Samuel to whirl in surprise.

"Enter," he called, and with great shock, he saw Nora appear.

"Miss Has—Chalmers, this is highly unusual!" he growled when she closed the door at her back. "You should not be here."

"I wanted to speak with you before you do something foolish," she replied without a modicum of shame. "Refer to me as Miss Chalmers in front of the others, for example."

Samuel exhaled in a breath of frustration.

"What will you have me do?" he demanded. "You have done poorly hiding your true identity as it stands. It is only a matter of time before the Balfours understand you are not whom you claim!"

In truth, Samuel could not believe they had not ousted her already. If he had so plainly seen through her lies, how had a man as seasoned as Charlton Balfour not?

"Not if you help me," Nora replied smoothly, clearly prepared for such an argument. As Samuel studied her face, he saw that she, too, had likely not slept well the previous night.

"How?" he demanded. "I know nothing about what Mr. Balfour

may have done two decades past! How could I possibly assist you in this search of yours?"

Assuming you speak the truth at all.

Samuel was not certain she could be trusted. Nothing but lies had sprung from her lips since the morning he had first laid eyes upon her, after all.

"You must know more than you say," Nora insisted. "Why, you are the maître d'. It is not the proprietor who truly runs the hotel but the servants who work silently among the guests. You must have tales, know secrets."

Samuel eyed her, mildly disgusted.

"You have truly not planned this well, have you?" he demanded. "Your disguise is poor. Your story is thin. You have not a lick of evidence to pursue. I ask you again, what brings you here?"

He could not be certain which was more disdainful—the fact that she had come so brazenly to the hotel or that he was considering assisting her.

"I want the truth!" Nora barked back, unfalteringly, and Samuel's eyes widened in disbelief. She was so bold, so unafraid. It scared him in a small way. She was inviting trouble for herself and yet she did not seem to care in the least. He cared, he realized. He cared what happened to her and he was worried for her.

The Balfours will not take well to a woman nosing about their business.

Inexplicably, Samuel felt a rush of possessiveness for this manner-less beauty whom he had only just met. Perhaps she reminded him of someone, but at that moment, he could not say whom.

Surely, not my mother. Mother was meek and did as was expected of her.

Samuel quickly dismissed the memory of his childhood and refocused his attention on the woman before him.

"You will not find any truths if you continue as you have," Samuel insisted. "You have not given me good cause to believe a word you have uttered."

"I have spoken with many people, former servants and guests who had come here. They all have the same opinion of the hotel—that it is rife with secrets."

"Gossip," Samuel snapped. "Rumors."

"So many cannot be incorrect, Samuel, and I know you are loyal to your employers, but you must not lie. There are many scandals hidden inside these walls."

"I know nothing about scandals," Samuel interjected. "You should not be here. If anyone were to see you—"

"I will not leave until you agree to help me find the truth."

"Why me?" Samuel demanded in exasperation. "How have I come to be your accomplice?"

"You speak as though I have some treachery concocted. I only seek to learn the truth about what my mother told me," she muttered, seeming embarrassed for the first time. "Need I remind you that it was *you* who involved yourself in *my* affairs."

Samuel felt his cheeks flush with some humiliation and he grunted. It was not entirely so but nonetheless, he knew she was somewhat correct. If he had not stolen her away from the family's table the previous night, she would likely not be standing in his bedchambers in such an inappropriate manner at that moment. Samuel could not decide if he was agitated or thrilled to have her before him.

"You must leave," he growled, hearing footsteps pass by his quarters. "This is ludicrous."

"I will not leave until you agree, Samuel. If I have the tenacity to uncover the identity of my father, imagine what I might do if I also look into your past."

"That is blackmail!" Samuel snapped, unsure if he should feel compassion or fury toward this woman. One moment she seemed plaintive, almost vulnerable. The next, she was threatening his security within the hotel.

She is incorrigible!

"You need only nod your head, Samuel," Nora insisted, and he could that see she, too, was growing uncomfortable standing unaccompanied inside his chambers. Perhaps she was not as brazen as she attempted to appear after all.

"I agree to nothing," he muttered. To his chagrin, she folded her arms sternly across the swell of her bosom and cocked her head.

"Then I will not leave and you will find yourself explaining my presence."

"If you stay, you will find yourself answering questions also," he protested, but he could see that he was far more concerned with appearances than this wildling.

"Fine!" he ultimately cried. "I will help you, but I will not do anything uncouth. I rather enjoy being employed."

"I would not ask anything uncouth of you," Nora replied, releasing her firm stance and clasping her hands together with glee. Again, they were bare, and Samuel sighed.

"You cannot continue as you are," he muttered. She looked at him in confusion.

"How is that?"

"Running about without gloves, wearing the same dress at breakfast and supper. How did you ever expect to be regarded as an upperclassman without the manners?"

Nora's pink mouth parted, a flash of indignation sparking in her eyes.

"I have done just fine thus far," she retorted, but Samuel shook his head.

"You have not. The Balfours may be too polite to make mention of your attire and your lack of properness, but I assure you, they are already suspicious of you."

Uncertainty replaced the anger in Nora's eyes.

"My family is not well off," she confessed, and Samuel sighed.

"I had not guessed," he muttered gently. "Never mind that now. I suggest you use the servant's stairs to return to your quarters. I will be along shortly to give you brief lessons under the guise of bringing your morning tea. Do not permit the guests or the family to see you until I have come for you."

She arched an eyebrow and for a moment, and Samuel thought she might argue.

"Who are you, truly?" she asked, surprising him with the unexpected query.

"I am Samuel Cassidy," he replied shortly. "Hotel maître d'."

She smiled as though they shared the most delicious secret and turned for the door.

"I suspect you are much more than that, Samuel," she chuckled, pausing to peer into the corridor, lest she be observed leaving such a disgraceful scenario. She intrigued him in spite of his inherent desire to remain impassive, and he chided himself. Lovely she might be, Samuel must take care not to be entangled in her web.

I will help her find the truth, and then she will be on her way, he told himself naively. *If she truly is the bachelor's child of Charlton Balfour, there was a good reason her mother never told the truth. Charlton will never permit her to stay. If there is merit to her claims, she will likely be sent away with a sum of money and ordered to keep silent on the matter.*

When Samuel had first come to Luton, he had never intended to stay at the Balfour Hotel. He had come with a very different intention —becoming maître d' had never been his scheme.

You remained because you have bonded with this household, he told himself. *You staved off one problem, and now you are enabling another.*

A stab of guilt pierced through him as he considered the similarities in the situation. Why should he help Nora when he had chased his own brother away?

The circumstances are not the same, a voice inside him chided silently. *Your brother wanted to ruin the Balfours for no sound reason. If Charlton Balfour truly did father a child outside his union, he is deserving of all the fire that might rain down upon him.*

With that, Samuel threw his wide shoulders back and stared at his reflection in the glass defiantly. Yet even as he attempted to stare flatly at himself, he knew the reason he was assisting Nora Chalmers had little to do with righteousness and everything to do with his growing attraction toward her.

No, he insisted. *I will ensure she stays within the lines of decency and does not upset the household.*

Samuel's only hope was that Nora would not breach that line, for he knew not what he would do if she did. With another exhale, he moved toward the door, straightening his vest as he moved and started in surprise when he saw Xavier Balfour, his arm raised to knock on the door.

"Mr. Xavier. How may I help you, sir?" Samuel asked, feeling remarkably flustered. He wondered if Xavier had seen Nora leaving his quarters.

"Ah, Samuel, good," Xavier muttered, gently shoving him back inside his chambers. "I need a word."

"Is all well, sir?"

"No," Xavier said firmly. "It is not well in the least. I have a particular task for you today, and I expect you to oversee it with the utmost discretion."

"Of course, sir. What is it?"

"No one must know what you are doing—including my father or brother-in-law. This matter is between you and me. Is this exceedingly clear?"

"Yes, Mr. Xavier," Samuel mumbled, not enjoying the idea of being the perpetrator of yet another secret.

"I cannot stress enough the importance of discretion, Samuel. If I am wrong and others learn what I have done, I will never hear the end of it."

"I assure you, Mr. Xavier, you can trust in my deference. What is it you require, sir?"

Xavier inhaled sharply and spoke in a rush of words.

"You will follow this Miss Hastings and report her activities to me."

"Sir?" Samuel choked.

"There is something suspect about that woman," he muttered, beginning to pace about the room. "Father thinks me paranoid, but I am certain she does not act as a proper lady should. What do you think, Samuel?"

Samuel swallowed the lump in his throat, somewhat stunned that Xavier would ask his opinion of anything.

"I would not know, Mr. Xavier," he replied.

"No, I suppose not," Xavier sighed. "Regardless, you will do as I say. Commission Joshua to oversee your tasks today and remain on the heels of Miss Hastings at all times."

"As you wish, Mr. Xavier."

The proprietor's son looked at him with raised eyebrows.

"Well?" Xavier demanded.

"Sir?"

"Whatever are you waiting for? Get to it at once!"

"Yes, sir," Samuel muttered, rushing from the room. It was not until he was in the kitchen that he paused to consider his predicament.

Mr. Xavier expects me to spy upon Nora. Nora expects me to spy upon the Balfours. If I refuse to involve myself, I will undoubtedly face consequences.

There was only one choice to be had—he would play both parts as if he were a thespian and hope he did not mistake his lines.

CHAPTER SIX

Nora skirted along the back stairs in the semi-darkness. There was little light on this side of the hotel and she relished the dimness, especially after her conversation with Samuel. Although she would never admit it aloud, she was embarrassed by his blunt address regarding her manners.

Truly, she had believed she was acting as the wealthy did but she did not distrust Samuel when he told her how wrong she was. She bore a smidgen of shame when she considered how she had fashioned his assistance.

She would not do anything to endanger his position with the Balfours despite what she had said. Yet she needed an ally and Samuel had been placed in her path, whether by design or accident. She intended to use his knowledge of the hotel to her advantage. If it meant creating a slight fear in him, so be it.

As she made her way back to the fourth floor to wait for the maître d', she found herself thinking about what had brought her to Luton.

She had been reared in Peterborough, her parents struggling to keep food upon the table for her and her five siblings.

Nora was the youngest, but even as a child, she had known that her father treated her differently than her brothers and sisters. He was not cruel precisely, but the affection he lavished upon her sisters was a source of great envy for young Nora. When Gregory Chalmers passed away, Nora seemed to feel the loss greater than any of the other children. Perhaps it was the lifetime of longing for his love that had caused such a hole in her heart, but even then, Nora's mother had made no mention about her supposed paternity. That had come when Agatha Chalmers had been on her deathbed herself.

"You must go to Luton," Agatha had gasped, "and seek answers."

"Answers for what, Mama?"

"I cannot help you, Nora, if you do not help yourself," her mother choked, half-delirious with fever. The strange words only enhanced Nora's confusion, and she said as much to her mother.

"I do not understand, Mama," she whispered. "Answers for what?"

"Your father...your father is in Luton."

"My father?" Nora had demanded with dubiousness. "Papa has died, Mama."

At first, Nora had been certain that her mother was overwrought with her illness, but soon she realized that there must be some truth to her mother's declaration.

Why else would Gregory have loved all the others so dearly and held back with her?

"Mama, who is my father?" she had pleaded, but Agatha had gone to her grave with the answer, leaving Nora to unearth it herself.

For two long years, she had sought the truth, catching snatches of rumors that she had never heard before, only because her ears were open now. If not for her friend, Christa, Nora was certain she would never have found what she sought.

"...fear the matter. You must stop fretting, Anne."

Nora stopped on the steps, her ears honed to the voices just beyond.

"I cannot help but worry!" another woman cried. "Why has the duke come, Patience? Without word to anyone? And with Lydia about to give birth?"

The dowager duchess and Mrs. Balfour, Nora realized, her breath catching in her throat. Why would the two be convening in the back halls where only the servants traveled?

"James has given me no cause to question his reasons for being here," Patience insisted. "He is my son, and it makes good sense that he would wish me near his child when the marquis is born."

There was a slight silence as Anne Balfour seemed to be considering the words.

"I do not like it, Patience," Anne finally breathed. "There is something untoward occurring. He stares at me as if he knows—"

"He knows nothing!" Patience interjected, the note of alarm in her voice unmistakable. "We must not discuss this matter here, Anne. What if the servants were to overhear? Or the children?"

"The servants overhear nothing," Anne scoffed. "We pay them a fair wage to become deaf. The children would not be caught in a casket using the servant's stairs."

"Emmeline might," the dowager duchess insisted. "Come along, Anne.

I would rather not congregate on the service stairs."

Nora waited until she heard their footsteps shuffle away.

What does Mrs. Balfour worry the duke knows? What secret do those ladies share?

She could feel the mystery lingering in every corner of the hotel, in each dark nook and cranny.

I will find my answers, but what else will I learn?

Nora tucked the information aside for the time being, noting that it might be important later and moved along the shadows to the fourth floor. She slipped the key from her purse to enter the quarters and looked about with a slight feeling of apprehension.

Someone had been in her chambers—something was amiss. The thought caused her heart to race and slowly, she glided into the bedchamber through the sitting room to check her belongings.

Xavier Balfour? Elias Compton? Who might have come to browse through my items?

She thought of Elias Compton and how he had eyed her with such wariness. Nora had only had occasion to meet him once while in Christa's company. That had been well before they had married and Christiana had moved away to work at the Balfour Hotel.

"Is there a matter?"

Nora shrieked and spun around, confronting the man behind her with outstretched hands.

"My word, Samuel!" she snapped. "Haven't you the good sense to knock before entering?"

"I did knock," he replied shortly, striding toward her. "You did not respond."

She had been far too consumed with her own thoughts to notice.

"Still, you may not enter my chambers without notice!" she snapped, her nerves slightly frayed. "I would not like to report you."

Samuel snorted at her and shook his head in disbelief.

"My, how you bluster, but you forget to whom you speak!" he retorted. Contrition and guilt touched her, and Nora lowered her eyes.

"You must stop fighting with me if you expect me to assist you. I will no longer tolerate your threats," Samuel continued, and Nora nodded quickly.

"Forgive me, Samuel," she murmured. He seemed slightly taken aback by her plea and abruptly clamped his lips together.

"I do not mean to be so contrary," she continued, raising her gaze to meet his under her thick eyelashes. He cleared his throat with nervous rudeness and looked away.

"Fine," he mumbled, seeming unsure how else to respond.

"I heard Mrs. Balfour and the dowager duchess consorting in the back halls," she went on. "Why does Mrs. Balfour mistrust the duke?"

Samuel's eyes narrowed into slits.

"What has that to do with Mr. Balfour being your sire?" he demanded. "Nothing, I would say."

Nora balked at the reminder and hung her head again.

"Perhaps. Perhaps not. I was told that Mrs. Balfour is quite bosky."

Samuel's face darkened, and Nora realized she had again said something to upset him.

"What?" she demanded defensively, although he did not speak openly of his annoyance. "It is a fact! Everyone speaks to her condition. She is a drunk!"

"This is precisely what I spoke of earlier," Samuel told her sternly. "You cannot speak so freely without raising eyebrows from everyone you encounter. You lack tact, decorum. These are not traits that one can learn by mimicking a lady from afar."

He paused and stared at her, his fine jaw twitching, and Nora found herself staring at his well-structured face with renewed interest. He was truly dashing, as if he was a prince disguised as a servant.

Perhaps that is why he has come here. He is pretending to be someone he is not—just as I am.

Nora knew she was being fanciful. No nobleman would be caught dead wearing the uniform of a servant. Samuel, too, was hiding a secret. Still, she could not seem to pull her eyes away from his face, as though he might confess that he was the heir to a throne in some destination far from England.

Yet when he spoke again, it was only to question her again.

"Whom have you spoken with that knows so much about this household?" Samuel demanded to know. She paled slightly, prepared to deny any such person existed, but she realized she had already confessed so much to Samuel.

"Christiana Wesley," she muttered. "She is the one who has supplied me with the details of what has happened here."

Samuel frowned as though the name was familiar, but he could not place it.

"Wesley," he murmured. "Who is she?"

"She was once a chambermaid here," Nora explained. "She is married to the former maître d' of this hotel, Honor Wesley."

Understanding flooded Samuel's face then, and he exhaled in a breath.

"I see," he murmured slowly. "You have seen them recently, then? Last I heard, they had disappeared without a word to anyone."

"That is not quite so," Nora confessed. "Elias and Emmeline Compton were aware they went to Cambridge. In fact, I believe they sent them on their way with a fair sum. There was quite a twisted tale involving Christa, and it was best that she went before more damage was done."

"I do not care to muddle my mind with ancient history, Miss Chalmers," he muttered, but Nora could see he was intrigued by what she knew.

"Is that a fact?"

"Is it," he replied firmly. "If Honor Wesley were still here, I would not have a job serving the hotel."

"Indeed," she murmured although she wondered if he truly did enjoy his status as much as he claimed. "Regardless, Christiana and Honor both knew the comings and goings of this hotel better than anyone."

"From years past, perhaps," Samuel countered. "Neither has been here in quite some time, Miss Chalmers. As I said—it is ancient history."

"You must stop calling me that," Nora grumbled, looking about as though she suspected there were ears within the walls.

"What would you have me call you?" Samuel asked in exasperation. "To call you Miss Hastings would be a lie."

She chose to ignore his dry comment and instead address the question.

"When we are alone, you may call me Nora. Beyond these walls, you will need to remember I am Lorna Hastings."

"You realize you are apt to get caught in this disguise," Samuel offered again as though she had forgotten his initial warnings on the matter.

"You have made your opinion abundantly clear," she replied shortly. "Is that not why you are here? To assist me so that I am not discovered."

A slight frown formed on Samuel's face, and Nora wondered nervously if he was reconsidering his assistance.

"Please, Samuel," she pleaded before he could say anything. "I will not cause you any trouble."

"You already have," he sighed but made no move to leave her chambers. "Shall we get started with your etiquette lessons? I have other matters to attend today."

His tone was sharp, but Nora did not miss the glint in his dark eyes, and it gave her a semblance of comfort.

He is warming to me, she thought, and the idea made her blush slightly, for Nora knew that despite the harsh and distant demeanor she tried to maintain, she was warming to him also.

Perhaps one day he will tell me his secret, too, and we will find we have more in common than he likes to believe.

Instantly, Nora was ashamed of her thought. She had come to Luton to find the truth about her father, not to engage in romance.

Yet even as she tried to reason with herself, a tiny voice echoed through her mind, whispering, *Who is to say you cannot do both?*

CHAPTER SEVEN

Samuel did his best to avoid contact with Xavier Balfour and had managed for most of the day, but as the afternoon sun sunk to invite evening around the trees embracing the yard, his luck expired.

"Where in God's name have you been all day?" Xavier demanded, his face red with irritation. "I have searched high and low for you for hours!"

"I-I have been doing as you asked," Samuel replied, loathing to lie to his superior but knowing he had little other choice in the matter.

"My word! Where did she go today? Luton?"

"No...yes!" Samuel replied thinking quickly. "She went into town."

"And?" Xavier asked impatiently. "What did she do there?"

Samuel swallowed his nervousness, wishing desperately that he was not put into such a position.

"It appears that she was doing precisely as she said—looking for opportunities for her father."

"Hm."

Xavier did not seem convinced.

"Dear Lord, Xavier," Lady Elizabeth sighed. "Wherever have you been? The baby has taken a fever, and you must send for Dr. Forrester at once!"

Worry slid through Samuel.

"Is young master James all right?" he asked, his brow furrowing, and Lady Elizabeth waved her hand dismissively.

"He finds himself sickly as the weather changes," she replied with a confidence that Samuel was sure she did not feel. "Dr. Forrester will simply prescribe a concoction for him and be done with the matter. If my darling husband does go for him."

"I will send for him at once, Lady Elizabeth," Samuel promised, spinning to oblige her request, but Xavier stopped him.

"You will do nothing but what I have asked of you," he said firmly. "We have enough servants to send for the surgeon."

"Then do have them go," Lady Elizabeth snapped with some impatience. "The baby will not stop wailing, and the nanny is quite at her wits' end."

Looking helpless, Xavier realized that he had little choice but to obey his wife but not without a backward glance at Samuel, one which spoke volumes to his sentiments.

"Hurry along, Xavy!" Elizabeth growled once more, any semblance of politeness evaporating from her tone. Xavier did not need to be told again.

"What does he have you doing, Samuel?" Elizabeth demanded the moment her husband was out of earshot.

"My lady?"

"You need not pretend with me, Samuel. I am quite familiar with the ways of my husband. He has had quite a bee in his bonnet for two days now, I have noticed. What is the meaning of it?"

"I-I could not say, Lady Elizabeth."

"I fear you lie terribly, Samuel. Please do not ever make wagers at the tavern. I fear you will not take the table if you do."

Samuel wondered if he were truly so transparent or if Lady Elizabeth was simply better at reading people than most. The latter was likely so—she had endured a fair amount in her few years, from what he had heard, but Samuel rarely paid any mind to gossip.

"I assure you, my lady, I have not a clue what you mean."

Elizabeth frowned slightly and eyed him warily.

"You would not do anything untoward, would you, Samuel? Even if asked to do so by the Balfours?"

"Lady Elizabeth, I serve the Balfours in any way they ask," he replied quickly. It was truly a surreal conversation when he knew precisely the crimes Elizabeth had committed to save her own family, but he, of course, did not put the thought into words.

"You need not do anything that makes you uncomfortable," Elizabeth insisted, sighing as though she saw that he was shielding her from the truth. "You are a good man, Samuel. Do not permit the darkness of these halls to corrupt you."

Samuel did not know how to respond to such a statement and therefore remained silent.

"I should return to my son," she said after a silent moment. "Good day."

"Good day, Lady Elizabeth."

He was relieved to be left alone and hurried off to find Nora again. Their lessons had gone much longer than he had expected, which was why Xavier had been unable to find him. He and Nora had been in her suite, practicing.

"You cannot hold a fork like that!" Samuel had told her, aghast. Once more he wondered what she was thinking, coming here so unprepared. Beautiful or not, her manners were atrocious and apt to call attention. It was a small miracle that Xavier Balfour had not pressed her for more details. He was hardly renowned for his decorum.

"Will you be tending to supper tonight?" Nora had asked before he left her quarters. There was no trace of the arrogance that she had shown from the start. Suddenly, she seemed to realize that she was terribly ill-equipped for her endeavor.

"I-yes," Samuel replied. "I daresay that the Balfours and Comptons will ask you to the family table again as well. The idea of an unchaperoned lady dining alone is...tasteless."

More shame crept over her beautiful features, her green eyes sparkling with a combination of gratitude and fear.

"I should not be here," she breathed. "I will leave on the morrow."

Samuel had found himself stunned at the notion, and before he could stop himself, he called out, "NO!"

Nora blinked several times, confused by his reaction.

"Pray tell, why not? If I am gone, you will no longer have to worry about assisting me."

"If you leave, you will never know the truth about your father," he reminded her, grasping at the reasons for his strong reaction to her leaving. It was ridiculous that he would act so. The woman was incorrigible, rude. He was tasked with following her while his chores suffered at the hands of Joshua.

Yet he did not wish for her to leave. Not yet.

He had left Nora with an idea in mind, one which would shift the suspicion away from her. Samuel had not told her that Xavier Balfour expected him to follow her and report. She was already considering leaving and, were he to reveal something like that, it would surely encourage her to run off. Samuel knew he must find a way to reduce Xavier's suspicion.

I must find her a chaperone. No decent lady walks about without a chaperone and no father would permit it, merchant or not.

That was where Samuel had been headed when he chanced upon Xavier and Elizabeth. It did not stop him from continuing on his quest, rushing to his quarters to change clothing. It was there that he found Antoinette.

"Where have you been all day?" the head housekeeper demanded, her face pinched in a scowl. "How dare you leave Joshua in charge of matters far too complex for him?"

"I am on errands for Mr. Xavier today," Samuel replied, stifling a groan. He had expected harsh words from Antoinette, but he had rather hoped to avoid them until later in the evening.

"What errands?"

"I am afraid I am not at liberty to discuss it, Mrs. Baxter. Is there a matter?"

"Indeed, there are many matters," she snapped in her typically brusque way. "The hotel cannot afford a day of disorganization, Mr. Cassidy."

"I fear it is beyond my control, Mrs. Baxter."

He stared at her, attempting to keep his composure, but her stare was nothing short of withering.

"I assume you have completed his service for the day."

"Sadly, I have not."

She grunted and stormed past him.

"Charlton should sell this monstrosity, for when I die, it will fall to ashes," she muttered as she stomped away. Samuel's brow rose with some interest.

Did she refer to Mr. Balfour as Charlton?

It would certainly be out of character for Antoinette to be anything less than proper. Perhaps anger had merely overcome her. In any regard, it mattered little to Samuel. He had to find a chaperone for Nora, and he had not much time before supper.

————

The house was tiny—barely a full room for the man to sleep and yet that was precisely what he was doing when Samuel allowed himself inside.

That is all he does—imbibe and sleep, Samuel thought with regret, tinged in irritation.

"Up with you," he called, nudging the slumbering figure on the floor. "Up you go."

A loud groan of protest filled the room, echoing off the walls as there was not a lick of furniture to absorb the sound.

"What in God's name are you doing here?" he yelled defiantly, raising his head to frown at Samuel. "Have they finally terminated you from the hotel?"

"I have a job for you," Samuel replied, again nudging him with his foot. "Get up!"

A blinking, bloodshot eye peered at him furiously, but a sardonic smile spread across his lips.

"Why in God's name would I take a job when you pay my rents on this castle?"

"I will not tell you again." There was a finality in Samuel's tone, which made the other man finally sit up and glare at him with naked resentment.

"You have some nerve rousing me from sleep. I did not get a wink last night!"

"No doubt you were busy at the abbeys all night," Samuel retorted, and his comment earned him a sly grin.

"Indeed, I was. You should join me one night. They have a new batch of fresh, young—"

"That is quite enough!" Samuel snapped, disgusted by his brother's perverse manner. "I insist that you move along now. I have a task for you."

"And if I refuse?"

"If you would like a proper bed in which to sleep this evening, I suggest you find a pail of water and shave that scruff from you face at once."

"Whatever is the meaning of this?"

"You must come with me to the hotel tonight," Samuel said, and the man on the floor howled with laughter, displaying two broken teeth.

"Dear Lord! What did you do?"

"What? You do not like this look for me?"

"Never mind that now," Samuel insisted, pulling on his arm. "Up you go."

"Not unless you explain what it is you want, Santos."

"Samuel," he corrected, through clenched teeth. "You must remember to call me Samuel."

"A travesty," he spat. "You have become an Englishman now."

Samuel glowered, his good nature dissipating.

"I had no choice," he snarled back. "You saw to that when you came here on your twisted quest to confront Anne Balfour."

"She owes us!" his brother snarled, and Samuel rolled his eyes in exasperation.

"You are worse than Papa," he muttered. "But I haven't time for this now. Ready yourself."

"For what?"

"I already explained to you—I need you to return to the hotel with me."

"For what purpose, Santos?"

"Samuel!"

"Fine, Samuel. For what purpose?"

"You are to become Joaquin, Duke of Castillo."

His brother laughed so loudly that the walls shook.

"It is not funny," Samuel growled, knowing that time was slipping by as he fought with his brother. "Please, Joaquin, when do I ask you for anything? You must do this for me. Do I not pay your rents? Do I not care for you?"

"You would not need to care for me if you would permit me to confront Anne Balfour about what she has done to our father," Joaquin sulked.

"How do you think this information is worth a shilling?" Samuel yelled, his patience fully expired. "You have listened to too many of Papa's tall tales and now you are exactly his replica, drunk and muttering about what could have been. I am offering you a kingdom for a day and you are laying about bemoaning the past. A past, I might add, that never belonged to you in the first place."

"It should have been our past!"

Samuel threw up his hands and spun to leave, realizing he had made a mistake coming to beseech his brother for assistance.

"I should have known you would not help me."

"Wait!" Joaquin called out, an amused lilt to his tone. "Tell me what it is you need."

Samuel exhaled in a sigh of relief and pivoted back around to confront his brother.

"Primarily," he started. "I need you to bathe."

CHAPTER EIGHT

Nora paced her bedchambers, watching, through the long windows, the sun slipping lower. Soon it would be time for supper but she had been told not to leave her quarters until Samuel reappeared.

What if someone discovered that he was helping me earlier? She wondered. *Or what if this is a trap? Perhaps he has changed his mind and decided that I am hardly worth the risk to his job.*

She found the latter idea rather difficult to accept. Samuel had been more than patient during their lessons, even when she had yearned to stop.

"I am not designed for this," Nora had sighed. "I believe we are wasting our time, Samuel."

"You are doing well," he argued. "Better than I expected, truly."

The compliment filled her with unexpected promise.

"Forgive my curtness earlier," Nora had sighed. "I fear you are correct—I did not much consider the repercussions of appearing here as I did."

"We cannot change the past," Samuel told her wisely. "We can only look to the future."

What future does he mean? She found herself wondering, her body growing hot at the idea that he might be thinking of one with her.

Do not be ridiculous, she chided herself furiously. *He can barely tolerate you. He is only assisting you because he has no other option.*

But as the hours had slipped by, almost without notice, Nora could not help but feel that Samuel was spending more time with her than he was obliged.

It is almost as though he wishes to spend time with me.

She dismissed the notion and continued to move restlessly about the bedchambers.

How long must I remain here? She wondered and as she thought it, there was a knock at the door. Her stomach rumbled with hunger, but she dared not leave.

"Enter!" she called out, rushing to greet Samuel. Nora exhaled with relief when she saw him.

"At last," she muttered, gathering her gloves to slip over her fingers. "What took you so long? I thought you had forsaken me."

A soft grin spread across Samuel's face.

"I daresay you are quite difficult to forget," he murmured. Nora blushed furiously at the response.

"I was garnering you a chaperone," Samuel continued. "It will serve to shift suspicion from you."

"A chaperone?" she echoed. "I do not need another person looking over me!"

"He can be trusted," Samuel told her sternly but she was certain she saw a glimmer of doubt in his eyes when he uttered the words. "It is pertinent that we curb the damage you have already caused."

Nora's back stiffened.

"I did not realize that I would be subjected to a governess," Nora retorted with some annoyance.

"The duke is hardly a governess," Samuel responded, and Nora balked.

"The Duke of Holden?"

Samuel chuckled.

"No, of course not. The Duke of Castillo. He will make his appearance this evening as your fiancé."

The words stung Nora to her core, and she peered at the maître d' with wide eyes.

"My fiancé?" she echoed. "I-I do not know what to say."

"You need not speak," Samuel reminded her as he had several times already that very day. "You must permit the duke to speak for you as a proper lady would."

The idea made her angry.

"I have a voice of my own," she argued, and Samuel sighed heavily.

"Why do you ask for my assistance if you do not heed a single word of advice?" he demanded, exasperation clear in his tone. "I am doing this for your benefit, not my own."

"Where is this Castillo you speak of?" Nora asked, ignoring his question. "I have not heard of such a place."

"It does not exist," Samuel replied curtly. "But the Balfours will not know that immediately. For all they are aware, the Duke of Castillo hails from Spain and is betrothed to you. He was detained on business."

"Is that where you hail from? Spain?"

Samuel's face paled slightly, and Nora realized he did not trust her still.

"It does not matter," he muttered gruffly. "Will you manage to hold your tongue for this evening?"

"What of this duke? Who is he really? What does he know of me?"

"Nothing," Samuel said quickly. "He knows nothing but the role he is to play."

"Why would he do this?" Nora insisted. "Surely, there must be a reason."

Samuel seemed uncomfortable by the question.

"He is my brother," he confessed. "I have been caring for him, and he feels it is his duty."

Nora heard a ring of untruth in his statement, but she did not push the issue. She was mystified that he would pair her with his brother, even in a pretend situation.

"There is only so much I can do without the means to purchase you new garments or hire proper servants," Samuel growled, sensing her reservations. "Why do you constantly protest?"

Nora dropped her eyes to avoid his penetrating gaze.

"I am not protesting," she muttered. "I am merely attempting to understand why your kin would agree to such a farce. If he is caught..."

She did not need to finish her thought, but Samuel did not seem concerned.

"He will not be. I will oversee this supper personally."

Nora's eyebrow arched in surprise.

"Will you?"

"Yes. If the conversation goes awry, I will merely interject as I did last night."

Nora was unsure that the plan was flawless, but Samuel had not forsaken her thus far. She needed someone in whom to trust.

"Please, Nora, you must come along now," he said. "The hour is late as it is."

Slowly, she nodded and inhaled deeply.

"All right," she agreed. "Let us go."

———

In less than two minutes, Emmeline Compton appeared before her, a warm smile upon her face.

"I do hope you do not intend to dine alone this evening, Miss Hastings," she said gently.

"I do not," she answered, forcing a smile upon her features. "I am hoping my fiancé will be along shortly."

Emmeline's eyes widened, and she cocked her head in surprise.

"I did not realize you were accompanied." She seemed embarrassed by the revelation. "Where was he last evening?"

"Miss Hastings, the Duke of Castillo has arrived," Samuel interrupted, shooting Nora a warning look. Nervousness seized Nora in a torrent. She wondered if she had already said too much.

"The Duke of Castillo?" Emmeline echoed, her brow furrowing. "I cannot say I know that name."

"He hails from Spain," Nora muttered, remembering the tale she was meant to offer. "He was detained on..."

The remaining words died on her lips as she saw a handsome man approaching. Overtly, there was little to indicate that he was related to

Samuel. Perhaps they shared a swarthier complexion than the fair-toned people in the dining hall, but the similarities appeared to end there.

"The Duke of Castillo," Samuel announced stiffly. "May I present Mrs. Emmeline Compton, daughter to Mr. Charlton Balfour, the proprietor."

The duke smiled at both women, displaying two broken teeth and Nora gaped at Samuel in disbelief.

How was anyone to believe this toothless man was nobility?

"Charmed, Mrs. Compton," the duke purred, taking her gloved hand to kiss sweetly. To Nora's absolute shock, Emmeline smiled warmly.

"Charmed, Your Grace," she replied, curtseying. "I was merely inviting Miss Hastings to our table. I had not realized that she was accompanied."

"Then perhaps we will both join you," the duke boomed, to the shock of both Nora and, apparently, Samuel as well.

"We need not!" Nora protested, gaping at Samuel. "I mean, you have only just arrived. I would like to spend time with you."

"Nonsense, Miss Hastings. We will have our entire lives to be together. I daresay, I would very much like to meet the Balfours."

The was an ominous undertone to his words that Nora did not understand, but Samuel's complexion was nearly opaque with concern.

"We would be delighted to have you," Emmeline smiled. For the first time, Nora realized that Emmeline did not have an aura of wariness about her. She was guileless, sweet dispositioned.

She may be my sister, Nora thought with a burst of near panic. She had been so consumed in finding the truth about her father that she had not stopped to consider the familial ties as anything more than a passing thought. The reality was abruptly startling.

Emmeline may be my sister and Xavier, a man who despises me, my brother.

Nora hoped she would not faint.

"Please do join us," Emmeline insisted. "We did not have nearly enough opportunity to speak with you as we wished last evening, what with the unexpected messenger calling on you."

"Most excellent," the duke cried, clapping his hands with far too much enthusiasm. "Where are these delightful souls?"

"Your Grace," Samuel growled. "Are you quite certain you would not prefer a quiet evening with your betrothed after your travels?"

"Samuel!" Emmeline chided him. "The duke need not be told what he would like. Come along, Your Grace. Our table awaits."

Samuel's brother extended his arm for Emmeline to accept, and the pair moved toward the family's table, leaving Nora to gape after them.

"You must stop him!" she hissed. "He is defeating the entire purpose of being here!"

"How do you propose I do that?" Samuel whispered back, extending her chair so that she might follow before his brother was out of earshot. "It is hardly my place to squabble with a duke."

"Good Lord, what is he thinking?" Nora muttered, rising to her feet and hurrying after her faux fiancé. Yet Samuel had no answer for her. He seemed just as perplexed by his brother's actions as she.

"This may not be a terrible occurrence," Samuel offered with mustered optimism. "He might simply distract the Balfours from you all together."

"Or adding to their scrutiny," she rasped. "Oh, this is a disaster."

Samuel did not have occasion to respond as his brother's voice rang out toward them.

"Come along, darling," the faux duke called out to her, his chipped-tooth smile widening. "We would not want to keep the Balfours waiting."

Nora cast Samuel one final, desperate look but he did not meet her eyes. She did not fault him for whatever was to come, not in the least. After all, it was she who had brought this upon herself. He had gone out of his way to assist her. He could not be held responsible for his rogue kin.

Begrudgingly, Nora joined the table and permitted Joshua to pull her chair out as the Balfours, the Duke of Holden, and Elias Compton rose to greet her. Nora had not noticed earlier, but Mrs. Balfour also sat at her husband's side, the dowager duchess on her left.

"Your Grace, may I present my family," Emmeline offered, going through the table, but Nora noticed that Samuel's brother seemed fixed on Anne Balfour, his eyes boring into her.

"I am absolutely enchanted to be here," the duke chortled. "How kind of you to have us."

"The Duke of Castillo is betrothed to Miss Hastings," Emmeline explained. Nora did not need to look up from her plate to feel Xavier Balfour's eyes firmly upon her.

"Odd you did not mention this last night," Xavier said bluntly. "I would think it would be a topic worthy of discussion."

"Oh, Xavier," Lady Elizabeth sighed. "That is quite enough."

The exasperation in her tone made Nora wonder if she had not given her husband a rather thorough tirade after their supper the previous night.

"The Duke of Castillo," Charlton Balfour mused. "How have I not heard that name, Your Grace?"

"I imagine you do not get much word from Spain, Mr. Balfour. Oddly, we get quite a lot of information about you, however."

The malice in his tone was nearly palpable.

What is the meaning of this? What business does Samuel's brother have with the Balfours, and why would Samuel bring him here?

Nora's gut clenched nervously, and she again looked about desperately for Samuel, but the maître d' had disappeared from view. A feeling of betrayal overwhelmed Nora as she realized that Samuel had not been attempting to help her at all but had instead put her in a worse circumstance.

"We do pride ourselves on being quite newsworthy," Charlton chuckled, but the Duke of Castillo did not smile.

"Some of you more than others," he replied coldly. "Mrs. Balfour, for example. She is quite a colorful lady from what I have learned."

A hush fell over the table.

"Why, yes," Charlton replied slowly, his face hardening. "Mrs. Balfour is quite charming."

"What makes you think so, duke?" Anne demanded, her voice harsh, her words mildly slurred.

"Darling," Nora muttered in a low voice, "perhaps you should retire for the night. You seem quite tired from your travels."

"I am tired!" he agreed, his tone raising an octave.

"Your Grace. You have an urgent matter that needs attending at once," Samuel said firmly, appearing quite suddenly. "It cannot wait."

His brother turned his eyes toward Samuel hatefully but rose with a sigh.

"Such is the life of a duke," he growled. "I shall return."

Nora could barely breathe as she watched him disappear, and she realized her hands were shaking.

"Do forgive me," she breathed, standing abruptly. "I must retrieve an item from my room."

She did not give the family an opportunity to respond before hurrying after the brothers. She found them precisely where Samuel had taken her the previous night—on the terrace.

"...simple thing and you cannot keep your wits about you!" Samuel was raging as she pushed her way onto the veranda. "I was a fool to think you could be helpful!"

"What was the meaning of that?" Nora cried. "Have you taken leave of your senses?"

To her amazement, her faux fiancé smirked unapologetically.

"You could not expect I would simply overlook an opportunity to confront Anne Balfour for what she has done," he snickered. "That is akin to putting raw meat before a feral dog and expecting him to stand down."

"What is your business with Anne Balfour?" Nora demanded to know. "Confront her about what?"

"It does not matter," Samuel growled sternly. "Off you go now, Joaquin. You have, once again, shamed me."

"Wait!" Nora choked. "He only just arrived! He cannot leave so abruptly."

"He cannot be trusted," Samuel retorted. "He is vindictive and petty. I was foolish to think that he would have let go of this ridiculousness."

"You promised me I would sleep in a proper bed tonight," Joaquin whined. "I will not leave without it."

"You swore you would not be a fool," Samuel countered. "Yet here we stand."

"Permit him to retire for the night," Nora heard herself say quickly.

"We will speak about this again on the morrow. He cannot leave so abruptly, Samuel."

"No! God knows what he will do when we are not about to watch him!" Samuel snapped. "He is no better than a petulant child, and I cannot commit the time to be at his side."

"I will not address Mrs. Balfour again," Joaquin grumbled.

"You see?" Nora insisted. "Send him to his room."

"If I catch you anywhere but in your chambers, Joaquin, I will cut you off forever," Samuel swore. "Do not think I will not check in and ensure you are locked away."

"Fine," Joaquin muttered. "Which room am I to be in?"

Samuel produced a key from the pocket of his waistcoat and handed it to his brother.

"Yours are the quarters adjacent to Miss Hastings," Samuel told him curtly. "Be aware of your surroundings."

He truly did not tell Joaquin who I am. He believes me to be Lorna Hastings.

Relief replaced the doubt that had previously consumed her, and the pair watched Joaquin skulk away in silence.

"What in God's good name was that about?" Nora demanded the moment Joaquin was gone. "And why would you bring him here knowing that he had animus toward them?"

Samuel's jaw twitched, and he met her eyes squarely.

"I had hoped his foolishness was over and done with, but I can see he truly is more like my father than I ever imagined. He will never let this go."

She studied his face closely, waiting for him to tell more, and Samuel seemed to be considering his next words carefully.

"You must not think poorly of me when I tell you this tale," he said quietly and Nora laughed mirthlessly.

"After all you have seen of me, I am hardly one to judge you harshly," she assured him. The words seem to give him the confidence to continue.

"My father's family was once one of much wealth," he explained. "It was before my brother and I were born, before he was wed to my mother."

"What happened?" Nora asked, her heart racing slightly at the confession.

I was right about him! He hides a sordid tale of his own!

"He was engaged to Miss Anne Clarkson of Cambridge, but she instead opted to wed another man—Charlton Balfour."

"Oh!" Nora gasped. "How terribly improper."

"No," Samuel corrected. "It was not, although my father led us to believe it was done spitefully."

"What happened?" Nora urged, intrigued.

"I know now that Mrs. Balfour had good reason to marry another. Her father, Mr. Clarkson, had done his due diligence into the matter and learned that the Conostoga family had no real means, that my grandfather had wasted all the family had owned on gambling and in bordellos. He was a terrible businessman, and frankly, he thought himself more bobbish than he truly was. My grandfather had fashioned the marriage, hoping that Mr. Clarkson's dowry would put him right with his accounts, but he did not anticipate that his secrets would be exposed before his oldest son was wed to Mrs. Balfour."

"How fortunate for Mrs. Balfour," Nora sighed.

"Perhaps," Samuel muttered grimly, eyeing her meaningfully.

Or perhaps she simply traded one fop for another, Nora thought, understanding his look. *If I am correct, Charlton Balfour is no better a man, even if he has better means than Samuel's father.*

"My father oft spoke of Mrs. Balfour and how she had betrayed him. Joaquin took his tirades to heart and vowed to avenge her treachery, regardless of how ridiculous it sounded. Sadly, Joaquin is quite fond of his cups and frequently mistakes reality with fantasy."

"This is how you came to be in Luton?" Nora asked, the story slowly forming in her mind. "You followed your brother?"

"Indeed, and managed to stop him with a promise: he would not have to work if he would simply leave the Balfours in peace. I have provided for him so that he could follow in the footsteps of our grandfather and become a bosky. He is no better than a tramp—unkempt, miserable, and without pride."

Nora heard the intense regret in his tone.

"Why was it so important that he not confront Mrs. Balfour?" Nora wished to know. "You have not any ties to her, have you?"

Samuel sighed.

"Of course, I do," he replied. "We are all people, Nora, regardless of class or status. The decision Mrs. Balfour made all those years ago was guided by her father and of no fault of her own. I could not permit my brother to breathe scandal on a decent household for no cause. It is not right. In fact, the Balfours have been nothing but kind to me. This is why I remain their faithful servant."

Nora's heart swelled with affection for the man, but she could read the misery in his eyes.

"I did not think he would be so brazen, Nora," he sighed. "I would not have brought him here if I were not trying to help you."

She smiled sadly at him and reached out to place her hand on his. Their eyes met, and she shook her head.

"You are a good man, Samuel," she told him softly. "One who puts the needs of others above his own. You need not help me anymore. I am sorry I have forced you this far."

His eyes darkened, creating two deep, inky pools, which seemed to draw her in endlessly.

"You have not forced me," he replied gruffly. "I am helping you because I believe you. If I did not think it was the right thing to do, I would not have."

A wave of heat seemed to envelop her body, but she did not lower her gaze.

"Is your name truly Samuel?" she asked. He cleared his throat and looked away.

"You are aware of my true name," she reminded him and he offered her a half smile.

"No." He paused. "My name is Santos. Santos Conostoga."

Nora's smile broadened, and she squeezed his hands comfortingly.

"I much prefer it," she told him. "Then I shall call you Santos."

"You must not," Samuel murmured. "If the Balfours learn the truth of who I am—"

"Rest assured, they will not. You have protected my secret, and now I will protect yours."

CHAPTER NINE

Samuel escorted Nora back into the dining hall where the Balfours seemed to be involved in a heated conversation. The table abruptly fell silent upon their arrival.

"Where has the duke gone?" Charlton demanded, any geniality abandoned from his demeanor.

"He has a pressing letter to pen," Nora quipped, and Samuel was impressed with her quick response. In fact, Samuel was beginning to find he was impressed with a great deal about Nora Chalmers. Who could have guessed that such a combative woman would invoke such emotions inside him?

"I believe I will also retire for the night," Nora continued without sitting. "It has been a trying day."

"Has it?" Xavier demanded. "Doing what precisely?"

"Xavier!" Lady Elizabeth snapped, but her husband's eyes did not flinch as they stared at her.

"Do stay, Miss Hastings," Emmeline pleaded. "I would very much like to hear more about you. Perhaps you will think me odd, but I cannot help but feel that we would be fast friends."

Nora cast Samuel a worried look, but she nodded subtly. Why not? She would learn nothing if she did not speak to the family. She could not run away every time they attempted to converse with her. Begrudgingly, she reclaimed her chair as he pulled it for her, and the men also sat.

"Tell us more about what you are doing here," Xavier insisted, and his wife gaped at him in disbelief.

"Xavier, mind your manners," she snapped, looking toward Charlton Balfour for assistance, but Samuel could see that his employer's suspicions were mounting.

I should have left it well enough alone, Samuel thought mournfully. *Why did I bring Joaquin here?*

"I would rather know about your fiancé," Anne Balfour interjected, her red-rimmed eyes glassy with drink. "Why does he speak as though he knows me?"

"I could not say, Mrs. Balfour," Nora muttered, reaching for her wine. She seemed eager to join Anne in her intoxication.

"You must know something," Anne insisted, and Samuel sighed. All eyes turned to him, and he realized he had not moved.

"Is there a matter, Samuel?" Elias asked, his intelligent eyes narrowing on him. Samuel's gaze flittered about the table, looking for direction. It landed on the Duchess of Holden, and she offered him a wan smile, but he could see she was feeling ill from her pregnancy. There did not seem to be a friendly face in the lot, and the knowledge sapped his courage. He and Nora had pushed their good fortune too far. On the morrow, Nora would have to leave before matters grew even more complicated.

"No, sir." Quickly, he ducked back from the table and moved to his post, reluctant to leave Nora alone but knowing he had little choice in the matter.

"My word, Mr. Cassidy, where have you been?" Antoinette barked at him. "You are needed in the kitchen at once!"

"Yes, Mrs. Baxter."

Casting Nora one last look, which she did not see, he hurried off to attend to his tasks.

Nora must leave, but I will continue to investigate the truths of these claims. We simply cannot do it while she remains here. Each moment that passes makes matters more uncomfortable.

He found himself in the kitchen where two waiters were squabbling about the roster, but they both fell silent upon his entry.

"What is the meaning of this?" he demanded.

"The Duke of Castillo," Franklin mumbled. "He has been causing quite a problem."

Samuel was filled with apprehension.

"How is that?"

"He insists that he is an heir to this hotel, and he will not stop announcing it in the corridor."

"My God," Samuel groaned. "I will see to him at once."

"Mr. Cassidy..."

"What is it, Peter?"

"Do you think there is any validity to his claim?"

"Peter, mind your chores," Samuel snapped, spinning toward the staircase.

"He seems adamant," Franklin confirmed, and Samuel turned back, feeling the temperature rise in his body.

"He seems ape-drunk, you mean?" he spat back. He could not have the staff spreading rumors like this, not when there might truly be an unknown heir to the hotel among them.

"Return to your duties at once!" he barked when the waiters did not move.

"Yes, Mr. Cassidy," they mumbled and separated.

As they had said, Joaquin was easily found, wandering the halls with a crystal decanter in his hands.

"What in God's name are you doing?" Samuel hissed, seizing his arm and marching his brother back toward the bedchamber he had arranged for him. Samuel knew he had no right to utilize a room on the fourth floor when he hadn't the money to pay for it, but he had hoped his brother would simply do as he was told, remain unseen, and none would be the wiser. Now, he would need to find the means to cover the cost of the chambers because the staff had clearly seen Joaquin wandering about.

"You cannot silence the truth, brother!" Joaquin cried drunkenly. "It will prevail."

Samuel firmly clamped a hand over his mouth and half-dragged him along until they were secured in the rooms.

"Have you taken leave of your blasted senses?" Samuel gasped, his words escaping in short, uneven rasps. "You will see me terminated! You will see yourself taken to the barracks as an imposter!"

Joaquin grinned at him.

"What would you care? You only remained in Luton because of me. If I were locked away, you would be free."

Samuel's mouth became a line of anger.

"I cannot say why I care," he growled back. "For it seems you care about none but yourself."

Joaquin's mouth parted, his eyes narrowing defensively.

"How dare you say such a thing! I came here hoping to avenge father and—"

"You came here expecting a bag of gold for your silence," Samuel interjected. "I followed to stop you from blackmailing a decent woman."

"Decent like Lorna Hastings?" Joaquin retorted. "I daresay, Santos, you haven't the foggiest notion what makes a decent woman."

"Do not speak of Miss Hastings again, Joaquin, or I will have your tongue removed from your mouth."

The older sibling seemed stunned by the threat and he lunged his head forward, his depth perception skewed by the amount of liquor he had consumed.

"You fancy her, this imposter you are protecting? Why is she so important and your brother is not?"

"Joaquin, gather yourself, and I will see you off the property," Samuel said, ignoring the question. "I made a mistake bringing you here."

He desperately wished he had heeded his gut and removed Joaquin at the first sign of trouble.

"I will not go," Joaquin wailed, his voice taking on the pitch of a small, angry child. "I have just as much right to be here as you."

"Joaquin..."

"If you force me to leave, I will tell them who you are, Santos. I will tell them everything."

"You would not dare," Samuel replied. His tone was even, but his pulse raced through his veins. There was truly no reasoning with Joaquin in this state. Perhaps it was best to simply stay until his brother fell unconscious from the drink.

"I would dare," Joaquin insisted. "Why would I not?"

"Every cent I make, I send to you!" Samuel snapped furiously. "If you oust me here, I will be as poor as you."

For a moment, the words seemed to make sense to Joaquin, but before Samuel could be sure, his brother smirked.

"Good," he said gruffly. "Then we will return to Spain."

"You may return to Spain!" Samuel yelled. "My home is here. My life is here!"

Nora is here, a small voice cried out.

"You are treasonous, acting like an Englishman," Joaquin muttered. "Stopping me from avenging our father. How can we be cut from the same cloth?"

It was a question Samuel had asked himself many times before.

"If you regard me with such contempt, Joaquin, perhaps you should move along."

Joaquin's mouth curled into a sneer, and he shook his head.

"I would never do that, *hermano mio,*" he purred. "You are my brother, and family remains together."

Samuel realized then that he would never succeed in removing his brother from the property without a fuss and without arousing attention. His heart was in his throat as he thought quickly.

"Joaquin, you must sleep off this nonsense. You make little sense, and frankly, you are upsetting the servants and guests alike. On the morrow, I will see you out before anyone notices."

"No!" he muttered, folding his arms over his shoulders and glaring ruthlessly at Samuel. "No, Santos, I am not going anywhere. If you stay, so will I."

"We will discuss it in the morning," Samuel growled. "And you must stop calling me Santos at once!"

A small sound caused Samuel to whirl, and his mouth gaped open as he saw that they had been overheard.

"Mrs. Compton!" he gasped. "What are you doing here?"

Emmeline's eyes were curious slits, her mouth pulled in at the corners.

"Who is paying for these quarters? There is no name on the ledger, but the signature is yours."

Fear plagued him.

"T-the duke of course," Samuel gasped. "I will check over the ledger. I must have made a mistake."

"Yes," Emmeline sighed. "I believe you have. Several, in fact."

Blood was draining from his face, and he stared imploringly at Emmeline Compton.

"Please, Mrs. Compton, there is a perfectly logical explanation for this."

"I believe I heard most of it," she replied quietly, turning to exit the chambers. "The Duchess of Holden is about to deliver her child. The family is occupied for the time being, but you will wait for my father and husband in the office. You will go now...Santos."

The door closed, leaving nothing but the sound of Samuel's labored breathing in her wake. When he could finally move again, he whirled to confront his brother, his face crimson with fury.

"Do you see what you have done?" he roared, but to his chagrin, Joaquin was fast asleep on the chaise.

My life is falling into pieces and my brother sleeps like the dead.

Oddly, his immediate thought was not of his job nor his scoundrel brother but of Nora Chalmers. With him gone, she would have no one in the hotel to help her. Or protect her.

Perhaps she will leave with me, Samuel thought, the notion filling his heart with a strange hope. She had truly grown upon him in such a short time, the need to keep her safe almost overwhelming him. Joaquin snorted loudly in his slumber and mumbled something incoherently as Samuel stared at him bitterly. It was truly his brother's fault that they found themselves there. If Samuel had not followed Joaquin to England, he would never have felt obligated to care for his bum of a brother.

That is unfair, Samuel told himself. *Your hand was not forced. You did it because it was expected, even if Joaquin is the older boy.*

His entire existence, Samuel had served others without regard for himself. First his parents, then Joaquin, and finally the Balfours. Nora made him feel appreciated, desired and not simply as a servant.

I will not rest until Nora has the answers she requires, he vowed. *Even if that is the end of my career and my brotherhood with Joaquin. Nora has come to mean that much to me.*

CHAPTER TEN

Supper ended abruptly when the duchess began to experience pains of labor, causing the family to scramble to her assistance. Samuel had not reappeared, leaving Nora to find her own way back to her bedchambers alone. She could sense something was amiss.

Samuel would not simply abandon me at this juncture, she thought worriedly when he did not call upon her in the hours afterward. She wondered if something had occurred with Joaquin and her apprehension grew.

I must look for him, she decided but before she did, she opened the adjoining door between hers and Joaquin's suite to find him fully dressed and snoring in an armchair.

Instead of feeling relief, more anxiety flooded her, and she hurried out of her quarters and into the hallway. The hour was nearing ten, and there were few souls about, none of whom she recognized.

On the main floor, she spoke with Byron, the night concierge, and asked if he knew where the maître d' might be. She did not want to sneak into the servant's quarters again, lest she be noticed, but where else to look for Samuel? Byron's wrinkled face twisted into a frown of concern.

"Is there a matter in which I might assist you, miss?" Byron asked instead of answering her question.

"Yes," Nora replied sharply. "You might tell me where I can find Samuel Cassidy."

Byron hung his head and fear replaced Nora's worry.

"What has happened?" she demanded, leaning across the counter urgently. "Is he hurt? Ill?"

"No, miss, nothing like that," Byron muttered, glancing over his shoulder toward the office. It was only then that Nora saw that candles still burned inside despite the lateness of the hour.

"Is he in the office?" Nora insisted, her nerves fraying with each word she spoke.

"No, Miss Hastings. He is—"

The door opened and Xavier Balfour appeared, his eyes glittering as he saw her.

"Ah," he cried as though he had found some grand prize before him. "Just the woman I was coming to see. Please, come in, *Miss Hastings*."

She did not miss the sneer in his tone, and her reaction was to turn around and run, but Nora had no doubt that he would chase and catch her if she tried.

"Where is Samuel?" she heard herself breathe. Xavier's eyes narrowed into slits so small, she could barely see the green of his eyes.

"Samuel?" he echoed. "So, you admit he is part of your wretched ploy?"

"What ploy?" Nora demanded, attempting to keep her voice from wavering, but it was impossible. Her position had been discovered, and now Samuel was suffering the consequences.

I was so foolish. How could I have permitted matters to get so far?

Tears of frustration filled her lovely eyes, and Xavier glowered.

"Come inside," Xavier growled, casting a wary look at Byron. "I would like a word with you."

"I cannot," Nora mumbled, turning away. "I must find Samuel."

"*Samuel* is no longer employed here."

The words were a slap to her face, and she whirled back around to confront Xavier.

"He did nothing wrong!" she cried. "He...he did not deserve to be terminated."

"He stole from this hotel and brought an imposter to act as your fiancé. I would say he did plenty wrong."

"He was merely helping me!" Nora protested but even as she spoke, she knew she was doing little to soothe matters.

"Come inside," Xavier insisted, and Nora shook her dark head of hair.

"No," she breathed. She had to find Samuel and apologize for what she had done to him. Nothing seemed more important at that moment, not even finding out the truth about her father.

"You will come inside, or I will have you locked away until I can determine a proper punishment for you," Xavier barked at her as she moved away. "The choice is yours, but I assure you, it is quite dank and cold on the subfloor."

Slowly, she turned back around and gaped at him.

I could not be related to this man. I was wrong to have come here at all. No matter what, I will not be a part of this family. They would never accept me.

Yet a flash of Emmeline's warm smile leaped into her mind and the mischievous glint of Charlton's eyes as he stared at her.

"Locked up for what cause?" she snapped, mustering the haughtiness she had learned.

"For being an imposter. I know you are not Lorna Hastings." There was a smugness about him that incensed and terrified Nora, but she did not falter.

"You are wrong," she muttered. "Is that why you have fired Samuel? Because you believe I am an imposter?"

"What is your fascination with this servant, whom you met just two days ago? Perhaps you have known Santos much longer than that."

A gasp escaped Nora's lips.

How did they learn the truth about Samuel? She wondered. Nora certainly had not breathed a word of it to anyone, but perhaps Joaquin had? She recalled how he remained in the suite, asleep and seemingly oblivious to the world unraveling around them.

He might be in danger, too. Did Samuel confront Charlton Balfour about my paternity? Did they truly fire him, or has a more sinister fate befallen him?

Nora nearly doubled over with the thought that Samuel might be hurt.

"You knew about Samuel's secret," Xavier hissed, stalking toward her. "You and he have plotted something together."

"Unhand me!" Nora yelled, yanking her arm away from him. "You know nothing."

"I know you are not Lorna Hastings."

"Show me proof to the contrary," she retorted, knowing he could not possibly have any. "Show me!"

To her utter dismay, Xavier's smile widened and he nodded.

"I will," he assured her. "I was hoping you could be civil and explain what brought you here before I have you taken away, but since you are being contrary, I will simply have you put in the barracks."

He nodded toward Byron.

"Take her."

"You have not proof I am anyone but whom I claim to be!" Nora howled as the elderly concierge rose unsteadily and uncertainly to his feet. "You cannot do this! I demand to speak with your father at once!"

Xavier whipped back about, his face contorted in fury.

"You believe yourself clever," he hissed, sauntering back toward her. "I warned you that we will do everything to protect the reputation of this hotel."

"Where is Samuel?" Nora insisted. "What have you done with him?"

Confusion tainted Xavier's cheeks.

"Done with him?" he repeated. "I told you—he was fired."

"I insist on speaking with both your father and sister at once."

"You have no right to make any demands, Miss Hastings. You are nothing but an imposter who has weaseled your way into our hotel for what? To rob us?"

"I am not your wife, Mr. Balfour," Nora retorted. "I have not come here to steal."

Xavier's face flushed with fury at the reminder, and for a terrifying moment, Nora thought he might strike her but she did not care. She only wanted to know where Samuel had gone.

"If you will not fetch your father, I will do so myself."

"You will remain where you stand."

Nora spun toward the stairs, but as she did, the double doors opened and a handsomely dressed gentleman sauntered inside the lobby, his brow knit in concentration.

"Mr. Xavier!" the gentleman called. "What a relief. What in God's name is happening?"

Nora bounded toward the stairs but Xavier's voice ran out, freezing her in her tracks.

"What is the matter, Miss Hastings, do you not recognize your own father?" he called. Blood drained from her face, and panic overwhelmed her.

Run! she cried to herself, but what good would that do? She was caught. There was only one thing she could do now, which was confess as to her motives.

"Have you nothing to say, Miss Hastings?"

"That is not my daughter," the gentleman growled. "That is not Lorna."

"Oh, I am well aware, Mr. Hastings, but she has claimed to be. She and a trusted employee have schemed against the hotel."

"Have her arrested, then!" Henry Hastings cried, and Nora pivoted slowly from her spot on the stairs to look at them.

"Have you nothing to say for yourself?" Xavier jeered. "You have barely stopped speaking since your arrival."

"I-I..." Nora inhaled deeply and looked at the man who might be her brother, one whom she had never known she had. She found herself wondering what she had hoped to accomplish by coming to Luton at all. The past three years had been consumed with searching for her father, a man who had no shame in being unfaithful to his wife. Christiana had warned her that her search might not end well, that the Balfours were not what they appeared to be.

Nora realized she had hoped to find the affection she had missed with her own father.

I see that there is no love to be had here. There is only heartache at the Balfour Hotel for anyone who enters. I should have stayed away from the start. Instead, I have ruined a decent man, the only decent thing in this hotel.

"Has a cat captured your tongue, woman?" Xavier barked. "Who are you and what are you doing here?"

She stared at him defiantly, knowing that she would not go free unless she told him the truth.

"If you tell me where Samuel has gone, I will tell you all you wish to know," she told him quietly. Xavier snorted.

"How would I know? He was also an imposter. I am certain you will both find your way back to one another."

"Xavier, what is the meaning of this?"

Emmeline appeared through the ballroom, her eyes taking in the scene with mild concern.

"Mr. Hastings! I was told you would not be joining us," Emmeline said, realizing they were not alone in the lobby.

"We have been fed lies by a liar," Xavier grumbled. "She is not Lorna Hastings, just as I told you, Emmy."

There was a clear expression of hurt on Emmeline's face, and Nora felt a pang of shame. She bore no ill will toward Emmeline, who had been nothing but kind from the start.

"Who are you?" Emmeline asked softly.

"She is looking for Santos," Xavier continued grimly. "I think they intended to rob us."

Emmeline cast her brother a wary look.

"I only just saw Samuel off the property," she explained. "He is heading into Luton, Miss Hastings."

"She is not my daughter!" Henry Hastings roared. "I am sickened by this. Why do you stand there and do nothing! If you will not apprehend her, I will do so myself!"

With that, he stormed toward Nora and lunged for her before she could move.

"No!" Nora howled. "You must not arrest me. I am Nora Chalmers, and your father is my father!"

Henry Hastings became a statue, his eyes hardening, but Nora's gaze was fixed on that of her siblings.

"What?" Emmeline gasped. "I-is this a joke?"

"She is a liar, Emmy," Xavier huffed, his face scarlet with indignation. "She would say anything to shift blame from her ways."

"It is not a joke, Emmeline," Nora whispered, and when Emmy met her eyes, she could see that the hotelier's daughter believed her. "My name is Nora Chalmers, and I believe Charlton Balfour fathered a child with my mother, Agatha."

"What the devil is this about?" Henry growled. "I have heard quite enough of this nonsense. Where the bloody hell is Balfour? I demand to speak with him at once!"

"Come along, Mr. Hastings," Byron muttered, shuffling toward the incensed man. "I will see you to a chamber and have Mr. Balfour visit you personally."

No one else moved, leaving the three to face off with the reality of Nora's presence.

"This is preposterous!" Xavier raged. "She has already proven herself a liar, Emmy. Do not believe a word that is falling from her lips. She has clearly come here to blackmail Father with Samuel's help."

"You are sorely mistaken," Nora murmured, stepping off the steps and onto the landing. "I do not care about Charlton Balfour, not any longer."

Xavier scoffed.

"Now that you have been ousted, you mean? How rich."

"No," Nora replied softly. "Now that I realize I have something much more valuable at stake than my true father."

She turned her eyes back toward Emmeline.

"Did Samuel say where he was headed?" she asked. "If you tell me, I swear you will never see me again."

"A likely story. If we permit her to go, Emmeline, she will do this to another family. We must apprehend her at once."

The women locked eyes, and Emmeline stared searchingly into her face.

"I could sense there was something about you from the moment I met you," she confessed. "I knew there was a connection between us."

Nora smiled sadly as she blinked away the tears forming in her eyes.

"It matters not," she said hoarsely. "I truly no longer care. I wish to never see this hotel nor its occupants again as long as I draw breath."

She did not miss the look of hurt on Emmeline's face, but Nora knew she meant it.

"I am sorry for all the chaos I have caused. I did not mean to upset your household, and I assure you that Samuel knew nothing about me before I arrived."

"Samuel was not terminated because of you," Emmeline sighed. "He has lied to us about his background."

"You haven't a clue what that man did to protect you and this hotel. He was the only good thing about it, and now he is gone. He tried to protect you from me, too, but you were all too blind to see how decent a man he is. If you do not believe me, I suggest you speak to his worthless brother when he awakes from his drunken stupor in a few hours."

Nora moved toward the door.

"Emmeline! Stop her!" Nora heard Xavier shriek, but Nora knew her sister would do no such thing. Emmeline was more level headed. She would not want the scandal touching the hotel. Xavier was much too hot headed to see the grand scheme of the future, but when his temper cooled, he would realize that letting her go was for the best.

In the inky blackness of night, Nora paused and stared up at the majestic hotel, which she had thought would hold the key to unlocking her dreams. Now she was breathless to leave it behind.

She knew she needed to find the keeper of her heart.

CHAPTER ELEVEN

How strange the world was when it turned full circle. Suddenly, it was Samuel, who was the man on the floor while his brother slept in one of the best suites the Balfour Hotel had to offer. Of course, Samuel was not truly asleep but staring at the cracked ceiling of the tiny house, hoping that it would not rain. He wondered how long it might take before the roof caved in completely. Without a pence to fix it, how would he and Joaquin live now?

Clearly, they would need to return to Spain, but with what money? No one would hire them as Spaniards, not now that their identities were known. They would be reduced to beggars on the street, dependent upon the charity of others, but the journey home would be impossible for more reasons than merely financial.

His heart ached for all he had lost, but it mostly ached for the loss of Nora. Oh, he wished he'd had time to tell her what had happened, but he had not been permitted. He prayed that she had the good sense to leave the Balfour Hotel and never return, but that would also mean he would never again see her.

A noise outside caused him to sit up on the cold floor and look about the dark. Again, he heard the slight scrape of the door opening.

"Joaquin, is that you?" he called out, his heart thumping as the glow of a lantern appeared at the threshold.

"You are here!" Nora exhaled, hurrying toward him. "Oh, Santos, I am so terribly sorry!"

She dropped to her knees and placed the lamp at her side to cup his face with her hands.

"Are you well?"

Relief flooded Samuel, and he bowed his head against Nora's, sighing gratefully that she was safe.

"I did not think I would see you again," he muttered. "It is I who is sorry. If I had not brought Joaquin—"

"Shh! No," Nora insisted, raising his head to stare into his eyes. "You warned me to leave. I am the one who is shamed. It is I who is responsible."

"It does not matter," Samuel told her earnestly. "I should not have lied to the Balfours. I had several good years with them. I cannot complain."

"You never complain," Nora laughed, but he saw the unshed tears in her eyes against the flickering light. She sat unceremoniously on the filthy floor, her fine dress dirtying with the effort.

"You must not sit there," Samuel told her, looking about for something to protect the garment. "You will ruin your dress."

Nora laughed hollowly.

"I am not made for this dress, as you well know," she reminded him without moving. "It will be a relief to see it ruined."

"You are deserving of much more than you have ever received," Samuel told her softly. "I am sorry you never learned the truth."

"I did," she protested. "I learned that I was looking for answers in the wrong place. I do not regret what I did, Santos, or else I would not have met you."

He cast her a sidelong look and saw that she meant what she said.

"I am tired of pretending to be someone I am not. They can keep their luxury and wealth. I much prefer this dirt floor...and you."

Samuel's cheek ran warm, even as he caught the note of wistful sadness in her tone. He longed to gather her in his arms and tell her that all would be well, that they might find a way still but he did not have faith in his own words.

They sat in silence, next to one another, absorbing the warmth of each other. Each was thinking of what there was to do next.

"Here," he heard his brother grumble from outside. "It's right..."

The door kicked open again and Nora jumped in surprise as Joaquin appeared in the doorway with Emmeline.

"Here," Joaquin concluded, grinning as he stumbled inside, reaching for a wineskin on the floor.

"What are you doing here, Mrs. Compton?" Nora demanded, jumping to her feet. "I told you I would not return. You did not need to follow me."

Another figure appeared in the doorway, causing Samuel to rise also.

"Mrs. Baxter," he muttered. "What is the meaning of this?"

"Do not stand on my account," Antoinette said crisply, entering the tiny cabin and closing the door behind her.

"What is this?" Nora demanded, backing up as though she expected an ambush. "Why have you come here?"

"To give you the truths you desire," Antoinette replied flatly. "It is high time someone learned the secrets we have tried to hide."

Her voice was chilled, but in the dim light, Samuel could read a softness in her eyes.

"Please, sit down."

"Off my bed," Joaquin grumbled. "That one woke me from a lovely sleep." He pointed at Emmeline before collapsing to the floor. In seconds, he was snoring.

"T-thank you for getting him from the hotel safely," Samuel breathed, unsure of what else to say.

"I decided I could not wait for the good 'duke' to wake for answers of my own," Emmeline murmured, her eyes trained on Nora. "I know now what you meant about Samuel. I know what he did for us, keeping his brother reined in."

Samuel flushed with embarrassment as he looked at Nora.

"He has been faithful and loyal to anyone he loves," Nora growled. "And you turned your back on him without cause."

"He is welcome to return to the hotel," Emmeline said quickly. "The decision was made in haste."

Samuel felt a fission of excitement, but just as quickly, it dissipated. He could return to the hotel but what of Nora?

"Samuel will not return to the hotel as a servant," Antoinette interjected and all eyes turned toward her in confusion.

"He did nothing wrong," Emmeline insisted, scowling slightly. "Why would he not, Antoinette?"

"May I speak now, Mrs. Compton?" Antoinette asked as she settled onto the floor herself. It was quite a sight, seeing the formidable woman on a floor littered with vermin tracks and whatnot, yet she seemed unfazed by her surroundings.

"I heard you in the lobby before you left Mr. Xavier frothing at the mouth," Antoinette sighed. "You are a very brave and very foolish girl."

Nora scowled.

"There is nothing to fear from me," she sighed. "I will not confront Charlton with my suspicions."

"You need not do that," Antoinette replied. "Permit me to tell you a story."

Samuel and Nora exchanged a look and then eyed Emmeline, who seemed equally puzzled by Antoinette's role in this tale.

"Many years ago, Charlton Balfour was a dashing, manipulative man, who was the most sought-after bachelor in Luton. He was the heir to a hotel, handsome, and filled with unsurpassed wits. There was not a lady for leagues who would not have sold her very soul to be with him. When he agreed to marry your mother, Anne thought herself the luckiest woman in England. She adored your father, and he seemed to adore her. They were well matched."

"I remember when Mother was...happy," Emmeline sighed, a faraway look in her eye.

"Ignorance truly is bliss, Mrs. Compton. Your union is blessed for Mr. Compton worships the very ground you walk on, but not all marriages are so blessed."

Samuel saw Emmeline's mouth twitch slightly, but he turned his attention back toward Antoinette.

"He strayed," the housekeeper explained. "Often and indiscriminately. It did not matter if they were chambermaids or duchesses. Charlton was always a man in need of validation from a woman, and Mrs. Balfour tried to forgive him for his indiscretions. But your father, Mrs. Compton, he made it a game in some ways, flaunting his affairs in her face, seeing how far he could push her until, of course, she finally went off the brink."

"Oh, Father," Emmeline muttered, appearing sickly. Samuel's stomach also churned as she imagined what Mrs. Balfour must have endured at her husband's cruelty.

"The imbibing began slowly, but she realized that the drink incensed Charlton, and she began to do it more, as a slap to his face. I do not believe that Mrs. Balfour realized precisely how bad the problem had become until it was far too late. She no longer attended to her duties nor mothered you or Mr. Xavier. She merely floated through the days in a drunken fog."

"Poor Mother," Emmeline sighed. "She did not deserve such a life."

Antoinette paused and stared at her.

"Your mother became a very different woman from whom she was originally," Antoinette sighed. "She did things that Anne Clarkson would never have considered."

All eyes fixed on Antoinette warily.

"Such as?" Nora demanded as though she sensed that the house-keeper was struggling with her conscience.

It was then that Antoinette stared at the younger generation, shame coloring her face for the first time since Samuel had known her.

"I also succumbed to Mr. Balfour's charms more than once, I am aghast to admit."

Samuel inhaled as did the ladies, their eyes bulging in unison.

"You?" Emmeline choked. "Oh, Antoinette..."

"Many years ago. I was young, foolish...and I truly believed your father loved me, Mrs. Compton. I wanted to believe in the idea that someone could whisk me away from this life, like a prince..."

"I understand," Nora said suddenly, and the words sank into Samuel's heart like a knife. Did she, too, crave such a life? He could never provide the life she deserved, he knew that.

"I am sorry for the way my father treated you, Antoinette," Emmeline whispered. "But you were very young, and we all make mistakes for which we are not proud."

"Some of us more than others," she replied grimly, and Samuel could see that the tale was not finished.

"Your mother, Agatha, was a chambermaid at the hotel, Nora."

"I assumed as much," Nora sighed. "She fell victim to Balfour's charms also."

A long silence ensued.

"No," Antoinette replied quietly. "She did not."

Confusion filled the room.

"How can that be? Are you suggesting that Charlton Balfour is not my father?"

"He is," Antoinette replied miserably. "But Agatha is not your mother."

Not a sound could be heard but the hiss of the dying flame and Joaquin's snoring.

"Your mother desperately wanted another child after your last brother was born, but she could not have another. You were given to her, along with a fair sum of money if she left Luton and did not return."

"Oh, dear God in heaven..." Emmeline gasped, her face ash-white as she suddenly understood. "My father paid her to steal the child he had in sin?"

"No, Emmeline," Antoinette sobbed. "Your mother did."

She buried her face in her hands and began to cry heavily as goose-flesh exploded over Samuel's skin. He looked helplessly at Nora's shocked face.

"She took you from my room one night when I was working late sent and you away with Agatha," Antoinette bawled. "I never saw you again. You are mine, Nora. My daughter. Mine and Charlton Balfour's."

Time seemed to freeze with her confession, and Nora felt weak. Samuel steadied her.

"What kind of heartless, cruel..." Nora gasped. "She has children of her own..."

"I begged her to tell me where she had taken you," Antoinette continued, drying her tears. "But I think the drink had eaten away at her mind so dearly by then that she looked at me like she did not know to what I referred. Of course, Charlton was glad the child was no longer an issue. I suppose that is why I have such a high regard for Joshua. He was born to a married couple soon after you were. When I lost you, I dealt with much of my pain by spending time with him and caring for him as I would my own. "

Samuel suddenly understood how the years had hardened and firmed Antoinette into the bitter woman she had become.

"Oh," Nora cried, throwing herself into Antoinette's arms. "You mustn't cry. You are not to blame...Mother."

The women embraced warmly and when they parted, Antoinette smiled weakly at her.

"So, you see, my dear Nora. You need not confront Charlton, for I already have. I owed you as much. I have made certain you will always have a place at the hotel with us."

She turned to Samuel, her smile wavering.

"And you, Santos, I have seen the way you look at Nora. I have secured your place at the hotel as well. And, should the two of you ever wish to marry..."

Nora whirled and looked at him, her eyes large and surprised.

"Could we do such a thing?" she asked, her voice catching. "I cannot foresee it."

Disappointment almost choked him, but he could not fault her. If course she could not foresee it. Why would she wish to marry him? He was merely a servant, a foreigner, a waiter. She was now an heiress to the most luxurious hotel in England.

"Of course, you would marry someone of better standing," he replied softly. "I would not wish a mere pauper upon you."

If possible, her eyes grew even larger.

"Do not be foolish," she laughed, shaking her head and causing Samuel more confusion. "That is not what I meant. I was questioning whether we would wish to return to the Balfour. Of course, I would marry you. Have you seen the chaos we cause when we are together? We mustn't deprive the world of such magic. No, I meant could we possibly live under the same roof as Charlton and Anne Balfour?"

It was a heavy question, made lighter only by the fact that Nora had said she wished to marry him.

"You must come back with us," Emmeline said firmly. "It is high time that the truth is revealed to all and that Mother and Father are forced to live in the mess they created. There have been far too many secrets lurking in the halls of the Balfour. The time has come to cast them out of the shadows and into the light."

Samuel eyed her uncertainly, but whatever it was that Nora seemed to see in her sister's eyes convinced her.

"You are not alone," Emmeline whispered extending her hand toward them. "And you will never again be alone."

She extended her other hand toward Antoinette, and the women joined palms to squeeze gently as Samuel watched the scene in a surreal haze.

The combination of emotions was overwhelming—dread, excitement, worry. Yet above all else was the love he felt for this brazen, sassy woman, who had lied her way into his life and changed it forever.

———

I'd like to thank you for reading this book.
I hope you enjoyed it.
Please view my other titles at:
https://books2read.com/amandadavis

Printed in Great Britain
by Amazon